"I can ... **aige began.**

"I know you're going to be angry. I know I should have told you before."

"Before?" True repeated. "But we got married today."

"That's when I started thinking about what marriage would really mean."

Irritation heated his face. "I thought this was what you wanted. A real marriage. Children."

"I do want that." Her expression was pure misery. "I think."

"You think?" Frustration sparked inside him. "So why are you prissing around here in that gown?"

"Prissing?" she repeated. "I've never prissed in my entire life."

"Maybe I should have called it teasing."

"I'm not a tease. I— Can't we wait?"

He pulled her into his arms. "What kind of game are you playing? Some kind of virgin-meets-cowboy routine? If that's the role you want—"

"It's no role," she said, meeting his gaze. "I *am* a virgin, True."

Dear Reader,

In celebration of Valentine's Day, we have a Special Edition lineup filled with love and romance!

Cupid reignites passion between two former lovebirds in this month's THAT'S MY BABY! title. *Valentine Baby* by Gina Wilkins is about a fallen firefighter who returns home on Valentine's Day to find a baby—and his former sweetheart offering a shocking marriage proposal!

Since so many of you adored Silhouette's MONTANA MAVERICKS series, we have a special treat in store for you over the next few months in Special Edition. Jackie Merritt launches the MONTANA MAVERICKS: RETURN TO WHITEHORN series with a memorable story about a lovelorn cowboy and the woman who makes his life complete, in *Letter to a Lonesome Cowboy*. And coming up are three more books in the series as well as a delightful collection of short stories and an enthralling Harlequin Historical title.

These next three books showcase how children can bond people together in the most miraculous ways. In *Wildcatter's Kid*, by Penny Richards, a young lad reunites his parents. This is the final installment of the SWITCHED AT BIRTH miniseries. Next, *Natural Born Trouble*, by veteran author Sherryl Woods—the second book in her AND BABY MAKES THREE: THE NEXT GENERATION miniseries—is an uplifting story about a reserved heroine who falls for the charms of rambunctious twin boys...and their sexy father! And a sweet seven-year-old inspires a former rebel to reclaim his family, in *Daddy's Home*, by Pat Warren.

Finally, Celeste Hamilton unfolds an endearing tale about two childhood pals who make all their romantic dreams come true, in *Honeymoon Ranch*.

I hope you enjoy this book and each and every title to come!

Sincerely,

Tara Gavin,
Senior Editor and Editorial Coordinator

Please address questions and book requests to:
Silhouette Reader Service
U.S.: 3010 Walden Ave., P.O. Box 1325, Buffalo, NY 14269
Canadian: P.O. Box 609, Fort Erie, Ont. L2A 5X3

CELESTE HAMILTON
HONEYMOON RANCH

SPECIAL EDITION®

Published by Silhouette Books

America's Publisher of Contemporary Romance

For Jacob Hamilton Blankenship,
sweeter than sweet, my baby sister's baby.

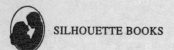

SILHOUETTE BOOKS

ISBN 0-373-24158-5

HONEYMOON RANCH

Copyright © 1998 by Jan Hamilton Powell

This edition published by arrangement with Harlequin Books S.A.

® and TM are trademarks of Harlequin Books S.A., used under license.
Trademarks indicated with ® are registered in the United States Patent
and Trademark Office, the Canadian Trade Marks Office and in other
countries.

Printed in U.S.A.

CELESTE HAMILTON

has been writing since she was ten years old, with the encouragement of parents who told her she could do anything she set out to do and teachers who helped her refine her talents.

The broadcast media captured her interest in high school, and she graduated from the University of Tennessee with a B.S. in Communications. From there, she began writing and producing commercials at a Chattanooga, Tennessee, radio station.

Celeste began writing romances in 1985 and now works at her craft full-time. Married to a policeman, she likes nothing better than spending time at home with him and their two much-loved cats, although she and her husband also enjoy traveling when their busy schedules permit. Wherever they go, however, "It's always nice to come home to East Tennessee—one of the most beautiful corners of the world."

Chapter One

Paige McMullen felt like a virgin with the vapors.

Though she had never experienced a Victorian-era swooning attack, she knew no other way to describe her current muddy-headedness. She could have blamed her sinking feeling on the sparse breakfast she had eaten six hours earlier. Or on the suddenly overheated air here in the Amarillo Rancher's Supply. But the real reason was the six foot three of solid Texas male standing right in front of her.

The weathered skin around True Whitman's bluebonnet blue eyes crinkled with his smile. "Hey there, Slim." He pulled the nickname out of their shared childhood history as easily as he doffed his worn cowboy hat.

"Hey, yourself" was all she could manage. In her fantasies, this meeting with True didn't take place between sacks of feed, with her in tattered jeans, misshapen sweater and no makeup, her hair scooped back in a ponytail. In her dreams, she was coiffed and perfumed and sophisticated looking, and her legs felt stronger than two limp pieces of baling twine.

True didn't seem to notice her swaying on her feet. "Is that any way to greet an old friend?" Before Paige could divine his intent, he swept her close. The hug felt natural and unplanned, the gesture of one old friend for another, an indication he was experiencing none of the awkwardness she felt.

She realized then that she didn't really have the vapors. For if she was going to faint, it would have been while she was being held tight against True.

Instead, her head cleared, and she savored the details of True's embrace. The way the January cold clung to his faded denim jacket. How he smelled pleasantly of earth and hard work, so different from the expensive aftershaves of the men who had populated her world for the past decade. How his face had hollowed out into interesting angles, losing the roundness of youth. The way his voice sounded familiar and yet new, deeper than she remembered, with his West Texas drawl all the more pronounced. And how she let herself cling to him for one long, sweet moment.

He drew back before her equilibrium could tilt again. His expression went from lighthearted to serious. "How's your dad?"

"Fine," she replied, but looked away. Lying to True had never been possible. That had been part of her downfall where he was concerned and why she had dreaded seeing him again. She was terribly afraid he might be able to look into her heart and see feelings she had denied, even to herself.

True touched her chin with two calloused fingers and made her face him again. "Is there something wrong? Has Rex had a setback?"

She shook her head. "No setbacks, True. No real improvement, either. Dad's the same. Just the same."

Those blue eyes of his gave her a long look. "And that's the problem."

She nodded, not really surprised True had read her thoughts. Her father, Rex McMullen, had been felled by a stroke in September, some four months ago. A strong and stubborn man, Rex had fought his way back from death's door. His stay at a rehabilitation facility in Dallas had restored his speech and some mobility, but the doctors said it was likely his right arm and leg would never function fully again. Though he was beginning to walk with a cane, some days he didn't make it out of his wheelchair. The man who could rope and ride with the finest, who had built the Double M into one of the most successful cattle and dude ranches in the Amarillo area, was forever changed. Sometimes the reality of those changes threatened to carve a new hole in Paige's heart. She adored her father and hated what the stroke had done to him.

"So you're home for a while?" True asked. "To help your father get settled after being in the hospital?"

She was surprised that he didn't know her news. "I'm home for good."

That rocked him back on the heels of his scuffed boots.

Paige laughed. "I can't believe the gossips hadn't already told you. I brought Dad home from the hospital a few days ago, and I'm staying."

"Tired of the good life in California?"

"It's hard for a Texas girl to find a good cut of beef in sushi heaven."

True raked a hand through hair as dark and thick as it had been twelve years ago, when he was twenty-one and she was nineteen and he had been marrying someone else.

Paige turned her thoughts back from that dangerous trail. "I'm going to run the ranch for Dad. Jarrett's still in college, and there's no reason why he should interrupt his studies when I'm free to come home, when I want to come home. My brother's got no interest in being a rancher, anyway."

"And you do?"

She bristled. "Obviously."

"This won't be much like running that fancy resort where you worked out on the coast."

Her temper spiked at his skepticism. "Of course it won't. Out there, I managed a thirteen-hundred-room luxury hotel with a full complement of resort features, four pools, a beachfront club, two golf courses—"

"Hold it, hold it," True protested, holding his hat in front of him as if to ward off an attack. "Damn, Slim, your temper's still as quick as a rattler's strike."

"And you're still quick to mistakenly treat me like a foolish kid sister." Their gazes met and held, and Paige wondered if he was remembering the last time she had reminded him she was neither a fool nor his sibling. She doubted it. On that long-ago night, when she had as much as offered herself to True, he had never realized what she was trying to tell him.

He continued talking about her running the ranch. "I'm not saying you can't run the Double M. But I never thought you'd want to. You've been gone for a long time. To hear Rex and your brother tell it, you had the cushiest job imaginable. And the times you've been home, you never said... You never acted..." He paused and shrugged. "I just never thought you wanted to come home."

He had little basis for reaching that conclusion. They hadn't talked in years. Since leaving Amarillo, first to attend college and then to work, she had visited many times, but hadn't seen much of True, even though he owned the spread next to the Double M. When they had run into each other, he had been with his wife or his children, and Paige had been accompanied by friends and family, as well. There had been no opportunities for heart-to-hearts, even if either of them had been interested in such conversations, which she wasn't and he didn't appear to be.

Since October, Paige had shuttled between the hospital in Dallas and her former home and job in Southern California. True had called the hospital to check on her father, just as other friends and neighbors had done, but he and Paige had never exchanged more than a few words.

As for her plans to move home, even her closest friends and family had been surprised. For years she had denied to herself her need to return. Her father's stroke had brought her to her senses. She wanted to be here, in this largely flat and sometimes unforgiving land. West Texas dirt ran in her veins as sure as McMullen blood. This was where she belonged.

True should be able to understand her feelings. He had never wanted to do anything but carry on the ranching tradition begun by his great-grandfather. So Paige just smiled and said, "This is home, you know."

He grinned and nodded his agreement. The unspoken communication between the two of them ended, however, as another rancher passed by and offered a greeting.

Paige glanced at her wristwatch. "Lord, look at the time. I'd better go. Tillie'll have lunch ready, and I have to talk to Dad about these—" She stopped herself before explaining that the sheaf of papers she held were unpaid bills she had just finished going over with the supply store's account manager. There was no need for True to know the Double M was undergoing some financial strain.

"Can't I buy you lunch?"

The invitation surprised her.

"Come on," True cajoled. "It's almost noon now, and in my memory your infamous housekeeper has never been one minute late putting a meal on your table. You'll be late, and she'll fuss. And Lord, how that woman can fuss."

Paige grimaced in agreement. "Tillie can be a pill, all right. When she gets wound up like that, I wonder why Dad has kept her on all these years."

"Most likely because she makes the best chocolate

cream pies in West Texas. The dudes go home talking about Tillie's pies and come back for more.''

"Forget the guests. Dad is the pie fiend.''

"He also knows Tillie loves you and Jarrett as much as if you were her own.''

"My doctor-to-be baby brother is her favorite. I've always been a disappointment to Tillie. She sets such store by appearances.''

"And you're just a pesky, skinny tomboy.''

Once more Paige wished she had thought to put on some mascara and lipstick and wear something other than her barn clothes. True would probably never believe Paige had grown used to sleek hairdos, manicures and smart little business suits. Being home always threw her back into old habits. Bad habits, Tillie would say.

To underscore the point, True reached up and tugged at the reddish-blond ponytail that curled over her shoulder. The action left her feeling about ten. Angry heat rose in her cheeks, and she stepped away, intent on leaving.

"Come to lunch,'' True invited again.

Paige tightly repeated her need to get home. She'd be damned if she would go anywhere with True looking as she did now. It was clear he still regarded her as something less than a woman, but she would prefer not to reinforce his misconception. The next time she saw him—

She reined in her runaway thoughts. When she'd made the decision to come back to Amarillo, she had promised herself she wouldn't be seeking True out or indulging in pointless wishful thinking about him. She had anticipated a meeting like today's, and she knew there would be no way to avoid him as she had on her visits in the past. She figured she would eventually get used to seeing him around. Just because the death of his wife had left him a free man was no reason for Paige to fantasize about him. Just because every man she met had been measured against True and found lacking was no call for her to think he would ever see her as anything but plain, old freckle-faced Paige Martha McMullen, his childhood buddy.

"I really have to go," she told him.

True let her pass, but he trailed her to the front door. He pulled on his hat when they stepped out into a gray and cold January day. "The temperature's dropping like a rock out here. Where's your coat, Slim?" He moved closer, as if to shield her from the raw wind.

Unsettled by his sudden movement, Paige almost dropped the papers she held. True leapt to grasp the tumbling stack before the wind could catch and carry them away. He stuffed them awkwardly back into Paige's struggling, clutching arms. The two of them swayed toward each other. In the process, his big hands skimmed over her sweater-covered breasts. Skimmed and, for one breathless moment, seemed to linger before pulling away.

Tillie had been right all these years, Paige thought with a dizzy sense of dismay. Ladies should wear bras.

But when Paige dared look at him, True didn't even blink, didn't betray in any way that he realized where and how he had touched her. Which was either a gentlemanly act or a comment on just how asexual she was to him.

Paige didn't pause to thank him for rescuing her paperwork. Turning toward a white pickup emblazoned with two entwined red *M*'s, she said goodbye in an even tone that was a triumph of will over pique.

"Mind if I come over tonight?"

True's question brought her to a halt beside the truck. Her brain started to whirl.

"I'd like to see your dad."

That quiet sentence set her head back on straight. "Sure." She wrenched open the door of the truck and slid under the steering wheel. "You're welcome anytime."

True stepped up to the truck and caught the edge of the door. "Slim, if there's anything you need help with on the ranch, you let me know."

Like hell, she thought. But she managed, "I'll do that," before pulling the door closed with a bit more force than necessary.

She drove away, determined not to check the rearview mirror to see if True was watching. But she couldn't resist, and a quick glance showed he *was* watching, standing in the middle of the gravel parking lot, his strong legs braced apart and his arms folded across his middle, as if he was in a deep study about something.

Certainly not about her, of course. Not her.

True thought about Paige all afternoon.

He spent several hours repairing fences in the south pastures. While he kept his hands busy, he tried to pretend his preoccupation with Paige was the normal interest of one old friend in another.

But his mind always went back to the moment his hands accidentally skimmed across her breasts. There had been just enough contact for him to form a fleeting impression of soft, womanly and unencumbered curves. His heightened awareness had been unexpected. And damned pleasant, as well. Surprisingly pleasant.

Of course, he had hidden his reaction. This was Paige, after all. *Slim.* His pal for the first half of his life. Oh, she had been gone a long time, and just before she left, things hadn't been the same between them. But nothing could erase the memories they shared. The horses they had raced over the flat, dry land. The wiener roast camp-outs conducted down by the creek. The swimming. The childish arguments. The fun.

The night Paige's mother had died, she had run away and True had found her. He let her cry it out against his thirteen-year-old chest before he took her home. They were bound by that night and a hundred others.

He hadn't wanted her to leave today. He had invited her to lunch because he wanted to talk about what she had been doing, about her plans for the ranch. Funny how he hadn't known how he missed her until he came around a corner in the store and saw her standing there. The years and the distance had been erased when she looked at him.

His wife had always insisted Paige thought of him

as more than a friend, but True had chalked that up to Marcie's highly developed romantic nature.

Marcie.

A brief, yearning smile crossed True's face as he climbed into his truck. Nearly three years after his wife's death in an automobile accident, he was able to think of Marcie without a crushing stab of sadness. She would be proud of that, he decided. She would have wanted him to get on with his life.

That earned a smirk. What life? He worked his land and raised his kids, end of story. Not that women hadn't made themselves available. In the past year, every eligible female in West Texas had been trotted out for his perusal. The matchmakers and the mamas and the women themselves had done their level best to get his attention, but he had dated few women more than once.

True shook his head, thinking of the seductive lengths gone to by some of these women. The slinky dresses. The candlelight dinners. A few had stooped to trying to win over the kids, as well, with gifts and flattery and all sorts of nonsense. He appreciated their efforts, and he truly wanted to marry again. But he couldn't imagine one of them sharing his life, making a home in a ranch house that admittedly could use some work, or mothering two children who would be ten years old next month. Furthermore, he didn't have the time or the patience for courting anyone, for hearts and flowers and all that stuff.

If the truth be known, he was damn sick and tired of the effort, of dealing with the whole process. And he didn't want to put the kids through it, either. He had gone the romantic route when he was younger, with Marcie. Now he would just as soon cut to the chase, find a companionable person and get married without all this fuss and bother.

He wondered what Paige would say about the women who were vying for the position of his wife. No doubt she would find them pretty funny. At least the old Paige, the tomboy hellion, would have laughed at them. She had laughed about Marcie at first, too. Laughed when True said he was going to marry a city girl and bring her to the ranch to live. They had argued about Marcie, he remembered. Nothing had been quite the same after that, and then Paige had left.

But now she was home. True grinned. He was pleased that she was back. Paige had been a good friend, something he had missed the past few years. Perhaps they could recapture their old camaraderie.

It was possible. Especially if he could set aside this unseemly curiosity he had developed about the curves beneath his old friend's baggy clothes.

Grumbling at his foolishness, True set off toward home. He turned his thoughts from Paige and noted with pride the tidy state of his ranch. The fences were in order, the barns and outbuildings in good repair. His herd was healthy, and a record number of births were anticipated in the spring. In recent years he had even branched out a little, breeding some horses for sale as well as cattle. Since his father's death two years before Marcie's, every extra dollar had been poured into additional breeding stock, building improvements and new equipment.

The Circle W didn't have the acreage or high pro-
file of the Double M, but True and his father had
brought the spread back from near bankruptcy to a
healthy bottom line. This year there might even be
enough money to make those much-needed renovations to the ranch house. Best of all, in True's opinion,
their success had been achieved without becoming a
dude ranch.

Not that there was anything wrong with opening
your ranch to guests. As Paige's family had proven,
there was good money in the tourist trade, but True
was proud that his was still a purely working ranch.
He planned to keep it that way.

He stopped at the ranch office and checked in with
his foreman, who reported the other hands were still
out repairing other fence breaks. As True headed for
the house, he cast a knowing look up into the gray,
leaden sky. The wind was no longer as fierce as before, but he smelled bad weather coming, snow or
sleet. That wasn't too unusual for early January, and
they were ready for a storm if it hit.

It was the daily storm True found raging in the
ranch house that he hadn't a clue how to fight.

His Becca, a chubby almost ten-year-old with
True's blue eyes and Marcie's gorgeous chestnut hair,
was locked in a verbal battle with her twin, Billy, a
skinny version of his father.

"You think you're so smart," Becca yelled, tossing
a cookie cutter at Billy. "Everyone knows you're
dumb as dirt."

Billy dodged the cutter and taunted, "And you're
fat and ugly."

"You take that back!"

"If you'll stop acting like a jerk."

"You're the jerk."

"You are!"

In a move he had perfected over the past year, True moved between the twins and rescued another cutter before it could be launched at Billy's head. "Stop it, you two. What's the problem this time?"

The explanation came from both youngsters at once, but True managed to figure out that Billy had ruined half of the cookies Becca had been baking for their dinner dessert. A quick look around the kitchen revealed the two kids had done their best to dirty every bowl, dish and baking pan in the place.

"Where's Aunt Helen?" True asked with a tired sigh.

"Hiding out" came a voice from behind him.

True turned to see his aunt coming slowly from the back hall. One hand held an ice pack to her head, the other rubbed at her back. "You kids," she admonished, her tone weary. "I asked you to wait before you started those cookies. Just look at this mess."

Becca's blue eyes filled with tears. "I was just trying to help you with dinner."

"Sure you were." True stroked his daughter's soft hair. "But when you're asked to wait, please—"

"All right!" Becca wailed as she took off toward the stairs at the other end of the room. "See if I try to help again."

Billy, who only moments before had been hurling insults at his twin sister, gave Helen and True a reproachful look. "Did you have to make her cry?" He disappeared up the stairs after Becca.

Helen lowered her stocky frame into a kitchen chair. The room was suddenly silent.

"I'll clean up this mess," True said, patting the plump shoulder of the woman who had raised him. "You've got another of your headaches."

She looked up at him. "It isn't my head that's the problem. I can't do this anymore, True. I can't keep up with them."

"They're going through a phase, that's all. Pretty soon—"

"Pretty soon you'll have to send me off to a padded cell," Helen interrupted. "The kids are out of control. They need a firm hand, and I can't do it anymore."

"I'll do more. I've been too busy with the ranch, and I've left too much to you."

"You're damn straight."

The gray-haired woman's saucy reply didn't surprise True. Helen Parks never had any qualms about speaking her mind. As a young woman, she had defied her parents and left this ranch to follow her husband on the rodeo circuit. Her Jake, as she called him, had been a champion roper, a hard drinker and a one-woman man. He died in the ring, trampled by a steer, leaving her with a nice nest egg and no desire to marry again.

Helen came home to the ranch just before True's mother died giving birth to a stillborn daughter. She stayed to help her brother raise True. Over the years, her duties had ranged from housekeeping to bunkhouse cooking to cattle branding. She had a fierce love for True and the kids, but she was now seventy-two. She didn't have the energy or patience she used to.

"You've got to get hold of these children," she repeated. "If you don't, you're going to have serious problems."

True opened the oven to rescue a tray of burning cookies. "I think they're normal kids. They make messes. They get into mischief."

"And you make excuses for them."

He shrugged and raked scorched circles from the cookie tray to the sink. "I try to cut them some slack. They miss Marcie."

"Me and your dad didn't cut you much slack, and you didn't have a mother, either."

"It wasn't the same. Mother died when I was four. I can't even remember her."

Helen sniffed. "There's no difference at all. Why, Marcie would have spanked their behinds if she had come in on a mess like this one."

"It's just some dirty dishes."

"Which you are cleaning up for them."

"Aunt Helen—"

"I'm leaving," she announced.

True had heard that before. "You don't mean that."

"This time I do." She pushed herself up from the table and crossed the big kitchen to the sitting area around the smoke-stained brick fireplace. From her sewing basket, she withdrew some papers, which she brought back and smacked down on the counter next to him. "Just look at this."

He found a brochure on a new retirement community in Lubbock, as well as a lease for an efficiency apartment.

Stunned, True looked up at his aunt. "What have you done?"

Her generous mouth was set in a firm line. "I've made a decision. One of my friends from the rodeo days, another roper's widow I've stayed in touch with, is moving in there, as well. We're both retiring. For good."

"But how can you afford—"

"For nearly thirty years, neither your father nor you has let me touch my Jake's nest egg. Even when you could have used the money, you wouldn't let me help. I've got enough put away to live out my golden years just fine."

He could only stare at her.

"Now you're going to have to deal with the kids."

"Aunt Helen, I don't want you to stay here just for them. I'll do more for them, I promise. I'll take a firmer hand. I want you to stay because this is your home." He swallowed, emotions nearly choking off his words. "Without you...it...it just won't be home."

Her fierce expression softening, she lifted a wrinkled, heavily veined hand to pat his cheek. "Oh, True. My boy. I'm going to miss you like the devil. You and those rascals upstairs. But Lubbock's just down the road a piece. We'll visit all the time. And it's high time I left this place to you and you alone.

I stayed after you married Marcie, though perhaps I should have gone."

"Stop that," he said stoutly. "Marcie loved you. She never resented that you were here."

With a practicality born of a life too busy for regrets, Helen shrugged. "It's true me and Marcie never got in each other's way. But I'm leaving now. And maybe that'll get you moving toward matrimony again. Speaking of which..." She turned back to the kitchen counter and picked up a pad of paper. "You had a few calls today."

True surveyed the list she proffered, reading, "Janice, Linda, Mary Beth and Tiffany."

His aunt cocked an eyebrow. "Tiffany's new. Who is she?"

He had a vague recollection of a redhead in a tight dress with long, lethal-looking nails, introduced to him by a well-meaning old friend. He shuddered.

"Doesn't look promising," Helen said. "Maybe you're being too picky."

"Aunt Helen, I'd just as soon not talk about this now."

Helen brushed his protest aside. "You need a wife, True. You're too young to be alone."

"But even if I do get married again, and that's a big 'if' considering the candidates I've seen—"

"You're just not looking in the right place," the older woman retorted, with a slow, mysterious smile that left True wondering what she was up to.

He knew from experience that she'd never say.

Sternly, she added, "At any rate, I don't want you

getting married too soon. It'll do you and those children good to have to deal with one another alone.''

Since marriage was nowhere in his near future, True didn't bother to comment. He was more concerned with her leaving. ''My getting married has nothing to do with you living here. This is your home. If you want to take it easy, you can do it right here.''

''I'm too old and stubborn to sit back while you take over my duties. I'm looking forward to just one room to clean, to napping when I want, eating when I want, maybe playing bridge when I want.''

True cocked an eyebrow.

She chuckled. ''All right, so poker's really my game. I'm sure I'll find some partners in Lubbock.''

She really was leaving, True realized with a pang. This was no bluff. What was he going to do without her? Not in a practical sense, but emotionally. She had been his ballast in every storm. Already missing her, he caught his aunt close for a long, hard hug. For the second time today, he was embracing a female who had played a large role in his early life. First Paige. Now Helen. One was coming back into his life. One was leaving. He couldn't help but think both were significant events.

Later, after cleaning up the kitchen and himself, getting dinner and smoothing things over with the twins, he set off for the McMullen ranch. He told Helen he was going to visit with Rex. He did intend to see his ailing fellow rancher, but in all honesty, it was Paige he was thinking about as he drove through the cold dusk.

The lights of the rambling Double M ranch house

were welcoming beacons in the darkened winter landscape. A long stucco and brick structure, the Mc-
Mullen home was larger and far more elaborate than
True's two-story house. A lighted courtyard served as
the formal entry, but as had been his habit since he
was a kid, True headed for the kitchen door around
back. He found Tillie Bass straightening an already
immaculate room.

Like Helen, Tillie had spent most of her life tending a home and children that were not her own. Except for their huge capacities for love, the two women
were quite dissimilar. Tillie was more than a decade
younger. Thin where her neighbor was heavy. Proper
and undemonstrative where Helen was raucous and
melodramatic. Yet the two of them were the best of
friends.

As she hung his coat on a peg near the door, Tillie
eyed True with interest. "Has Helen told you her big
news?"

True laughed. "I should have known she'd tell you
first."

Tillie's thin face looked more pinched than ever.
"I'm going to miss her."

Taken aback by what was for Tillie a supremely
emotional statement, True didn't notice anyone else
enter the room. Even when he saw the woman who
paused in the doorway, it took a moment for him to
recognize Paige.

In dark blue wool pants and soft matching sweater,
her strawberry blond hair loose about her shoulders,
her face just touched with makeup, Paige didn't look
like herself. At least not like the Paige he remem-

bered. Or even the Paige he had run into at the supply store today. Those curves he had imagined had been no illusion. She was still slender enough to keep her nickname, but she had developed in plenty of interesting ways and places. Even her face had filled out, caught up with her big, brown eyes. Now why hadn't he noticed that this morning?

He gaped at Paige until Tillie cleared her throat. Even then, all he could say was her name.

She smiled. "I should have known you'd come in the back door. What are you doing, trying to wheedle pie out of Tillie, just like old times?"

Filling the silence left by True's failure to reply, Tillie said, "He just got here."

Paige turned to lead the way from the kitchen. "You'll want to see Dad."

True nodded mutely, but didn't move.

With an uncharacteristic chuckle, Tillie gave him a gentle push toward the door. "What's the matter, True? I haven't seen you at such a loss for words since the time you tried to ride Mr. Rex's horse and wound up with a busted rib."

That was exactly how he was feeling, True realized. Like a would-be bronco rider flung flat to the ground. This Paige, so like herself and yet so intriguingly different, had thrown him, but good.

Paige heard Tillie's comment and couldn't suppress a smile. When she had changed for dinner, she had tried telling herself her clothing choice had nothing to do with True. What a lie. She had hoped he would come over to visit her father and see her in a more

flattering light than this morning. The stupefied look
on his face showed she had succeeded.

"Daddy," she called as she entered her father's
mahogany paneled study. "Look who's here."

Rex McMullen, who was propped up on a
leather-upholstered sofa in front of a cheerful fire,
smiled as True came forward with a hand outstretched. The right side of Rex's smile didn't quite
match the left, and he reached out with his left hand,
keeping his right beneath the afghan spread over his
legs. He was thin, his normally weather-bronzed skin
pale, but his shoulders were still broad and held
straight. His red-gold hair had gone mostly silver.
Paige thought the gray enhanced his ruggedly handsome features. She was prejudiced, of course, and
she'd had time to adjust to the changes in him. She
looked quickly at True, wondering how he would react.

If True found anything amiss about Rex's appearance, he didn't show it. Looking natural as could be,
he sat down in the wing chair next to the sofa. "It's
damn good to see you at home, Rex."

The older man's reply was a bit slow, but still
hearty. "It's good to be here."

Relieved, Paige left them talking about beef prices
and winter feeding programs and went back to the
kitchen, where Tillie was preparing a coffee tray.

"You read my mind." Paige opened the refrigerator and took out one of Tillie's famous cream pies.

The older woman set a stack of dessert plates on
the table. "Reading your mind's not so hard."

The dry comment begged a reply, but Paige chose

to ignore it. She concentrated instead on placing pie slices on the plates. "Do we need cream and sugar?"

Tillie snorted as she added forks to the tray. "Since when would True Whitman be the kind of man who waters down good coffee?"

Paige said nothing, always the wisest course of action with Tillie.

"True's the kind of man a lot of women want," Tillie added.

Paige nodded.

"But so far he hasn't been interested in any of the women who have been after him." The older woman paused long enough for Paige to comment, but plunged ahead when she didn't. "Helen says he's had all kinds of chances to get married again. She worries about him and the kids. Especially now that she's leaving." Over dinner Tillie had told Paige and Rex about Helen's retirement plans.

Paige settled two of the pie plates on the tray and carefully avoided looking at Tillie. "With all the talking you and Helen do, how come she hadn't told True I was home to stay?"

Tillie made a great show of wiping her hands on her starched white apron. "You know I don't talk about this family's business. Even to Helen."

Paige knew nothing of the sort. Disagreeing with Tillie would, however, be a pointless exercise. Paige just picked up the coffee tray. "Grab those other pie plates, will you?"

The housekeeper obeyed. As the two of them exited the kitchen, Tillie murmured, "That blue outfit was a good choice for tonight, Paige. You're real pretty when you try.''

Coffee cups rattled as Paige stumbled. Compliments from this woman were as rare as snow in July.

Tillie clucked her disapproval. ''Land sakes, child, be careful of your mother's best china. You'll be wanting to use it after you're married.''

For the better part of twenty years, Tillie had been telling Paige she would never land a man. So her quiet comment that Paige would be needing her mother's china came as another big surprise. What was this—a belated attempt at instilling some confidence in Paige's womanly wiles?

Questions were forgotten, however, when the women reached the study. True leapt to his feet and took the heavy tray from Paige, just as if he had been watching for her return. He was flatteringly attentive as she served coffee and pie. When she mentioned the room had grown cool, he was quick to add another log to the fire and draw the curtains against a cold draft.

He kept looking at her. Studying her, Paige thought, as if she were a stranger. When she tucked the afghan more securely over her father's legs, True was watching. When she folded the linen napkins and placed them back on the tray, his gaze followed her every move. When she laughed at Tillie's description of a dude's encounter with a stubborn mare, True was silent, his jaw propped against the heel of one hand as he scrutinized her.

Paige's reaction to his interest wavered somewhere between pleasure and panic. What was he thinking?

Once the coffee and pie were gone, Rex announced he was tired. While Paige gave him a hand getting to bed, True carried the coffee tray to the kitchen. Paige expected True to leave from there, but when she returned to the study, he was gazing thoughtfully down at the fire.

He suited the room, she thought. Just like her father. Both of them were big men. Simple in their tastes. The polished wood, leather upholstery and muted reds and golds of the study's decor were the right background for confident, completely masculine men. But then, she couldn't imagine a setting where they wouldn't be at ease, because they were at ease with themselves, first and foremost. Maybe that was why she was struggling so with the changes in her father. Because he was still adjusting to his new capabilities and problems.

She wavered for a moment in the doorway before True turned to face her. "You're here," she said, rather unnecessarily.

"You want me to leave?"

"Of course not. I just thought you were with Tillie."

"She threw me out of her kitchen, said I might break your mother's china."

"She's awfully worried about those dishes tonight."

True looked puzzled.

"Never mind," Paige told him with a wave of her hand. "Is there something you wanted to talk to me about?"

"I think so."

His hesitation was uncharacteristic. Once again his steady blue-eyed gaze was centered on her. To keep from fidgeting under his regard, Paige folded the afghan and straightened magazines on the coffee table. After that there was nothing left to do but sit down. Still True watched her, and her patience wore thin.

"What are you looking at?"

He blinked. "Looking at?"

"Do I have chocolate pie on my chin or something? You just keep staring at me."

His smile was slow and somewhat sheepish. "I'm staring because I never knew you were this pretty."

Her protest was automatic. "I'm not pretty."

"Are, too," he teased, just as he might have when they were kids. "When did it happen?"

"Pardon me?"

"I missed you growing up."

"I'm thirty-one years old, True. I grew up a long time ago."

"But when you left here you were a kid. All skinny arms and legs. Freckles and pigtails. Just a little girl."

"That's just the way you saw me," Paige said. "I wasn't a little girl at all."

True frowned, looked as if he was about to protest, then reconsidered. "You're right, I suppose. I wasn't very good at seeing you had grown up. And when you came home on visits—"

"You were busy with your family, as you should have been." She settled back into the corner of the sofa and played with the tassels on a pillow instead of looking at True. "That reminds me of how rude I've been in not asking about the twins."

His smile was immediate. "They're a handful at times, but they're good kids, all in all."

She spared him a glance. "I'm sure you're doing a fine job with them."

"With Aunt Helen's help. God knows what I'll do without her."

She nodded, and her next comment flew out of her mouth without any thought. "Tillie says every eligible woman in the county is offering to give you a hand."

He laughed, stepping away from the fire. "A few who aren't eligible have come around, as well."

Paige wasn't sure where her flirtatious giggle came from. "I guess they consider you quite a catch."

"What about you?" True asked, a roguish gleam in his eyes. "Do you think I'm a catch?"

Suddenly nervous, she again focused on the pillow tassel.

"What if I wanted you to think I was a catch?"

The question was spoken in such low tones Paige wasn't sure she had heard him correctly.

He didn't help her out by repeating it. Instead, he asked another question that took her by surprise. "How come you're not married, Paige?"

She blinked. "What kind of thing is that to ask?"

"I just wondered. Don't you want to be married?"

None of your business, she thought before evading the question. "Right now I just want to get the ranch shaped up."

His eyebrows drew together in concern. "Is there a problem?"

"Nothing that having someone firmly in control

won't solve. Dad's been gone for four months, and from the looks of things, he wasn't feeling his best before then. The ranch foreman has been given too much freedom and responsibility, and we've got a lot of work to do if we're going to be ready for the guests we expect this spring."

True pursed his lips, his expression thoughtful. "Are you sure you've done the right thing coming back here?"

Paige pushed herself to her feet. "What is this? The West Texas version of the Spanish Inquisition?"

"You're biting off a big job here." He held up his hand when she started a protest. "Now don't get all riled up like you did this morning. I'm not implying it's a job you can't do."

Sure that's what he was implying, she managed to hold on to her temper. "Look here, True. I've been dreaming of home for a long, long time. I'm never leaving again, if I can help it."

Again True's slow grin appeared. "So if you get married, it better be someone who respects your love of this place."

"I suppose," she snapped. "But I'm not thinking of getting married anytime soon."

"Not even to me?"

His question hit her like a streak of lightning. The room went all blue and white and electric.

And suddenly True had left the fire and was standing beside her, taking her hand, looking down at her with his expression serious and intense.

"I think we ought to get married, Paige. I think it makes a whole lot of sense."

Sense? For the life of her, Paige couldn't figure out what a crazy man was doing talking about sense.

She snatched her hands back and demanded, "What kind of damned fool joke are you pulling, William True Whitman?"

"No joke, Slim." Sure enough, his gaze was steady and solemn, as far from teasing as you could get. So was his voice when he asked, "Will you marry me?"

Chapter Two

Snow came in the night, covering the ground like the white, sugary frosting on Aunt Helen's special Christmas cakes. Since the temperature wasn't all that cold and the sky promised a fair day, True figured the frozen coating would melt by afternoon. All the more reason for him to saddle Goldie and enjoy an early morning ride. The harsh land was pretty in the snow, gentled by the frozen mantle. Quiet, too. A man could hear his thoughts clearly in the silence. True had always done his best thinking on horseback, and since he had plenty to mull over, the snow-covered landscape provided a welcome haven.

Last night, Paige had said no to his proposal. That was her first reaction, at any rate. She had been so shocked all she could do was sputter, shake her head and back away as if he were some kind of mad scientist who had suggested transplanting her brain. In fact, when she could talk, she had suggested his brain had taken a hike.

But then True had looked down into those dark eyes of hers. Eyes as velvety brown as sunflower hearts. Right then, he had known she wanted to marry him. No matter what Paige said, her eyes couldn't lie to him.

Neither could her kiss.

At that particular memory, True drew his palomino to a halt at the creek that bordered the west edge of his property and separated his ranch from the Double M. He stared down at the cold, clear water, but what he saw was Paige's face just before he kissed her. A face full of expectation and reluctant yearning.

He hadn't put any thought into kissing her. No, now that was a lie, his conscience reminded him. He first thought of kissing Paige when he watched her eat pie. The glide of her lips over the fork had fascinated him. The way her mouth pursed with pleasure. How her pink tongue rescued a dollop of meringue from the corner of her lips. He had wanted to kiss her right then, and the impulse had astounded him almost as much as the fact that Paige had become an attractive, alluring woman.

Alluring, yes. And still the same Paige he knew so well.

It was that combination which had hit him square between the eyes sometime between when she served the pie and Rex decided to go to bed. She was sexy and attractive, and yet she was as familiar to him as his own reflection. It was an appealing combination that no other woman of True's acquaintance could offer.

Paige wouldn't have to try to understand his deep affection for the land or the backbreaking work it took to ranch. They shared a heritage that couldn't be learned. Even some people born to this land—like Paige's younger brother, Jarrett—didn't feel the kinship True and Paige felt for their homes. Paige had tried living elsewhere, but she was back. And unless True was badly misjudging the resolve in her, this wasn't a decision she had made lightly. She was home to stay.

And he wanted her.

Aunt Helen had planted the seed of his proposal. Yesterday, she had said he wasn't looking in the right place for a wife. As usual, the woman was on target. All True had to do was look next door and see, *really* see, Paige McMullen.

Last night he had watched her solicitous manner with her father and with him, the womanly way she tended to little things like coffee and fine napkins. She had filled any lull in the conversation with sudden, sweet smiles. She applied herself to the comfort of everyone in much the same way she had once applied herself to mastering a horseback riding trick. Despite the fact that Tillie had once despaired of turning her into a lady, Paige had absorbed those lessons well. She was caring and courteous, gentle and soothing. Yet he figured she could probably still rope a steer with the same aplomb as she entertained with pretty china and gracious airs.

He didn't just want her; he needed her.

True had made his decision quickly. All he had to do was compare the lovely and intelligent woman that Paige was to the series of overeager matrimonial prospects who had been paraded out for his inspection over the past year or so. There was no contest. Paige won.

They were perfect for each other. She had protested when he told her that, so he had kissed her. He hadn't known where the kiss would go, but he was surprised by the way it deepened and strengthened, how curiosity turned easily to desire.

He realized then that he could lose himself in her. Immerse himself in the scent of her subtly feminine perfume. Linger over the curves that fit against him so well. His body had stirred in response to the kiss, to her. To Paige.

He remembered she finally drew away from the kiss with a halfhearted shove. "What in the hell are you doing?"

"Kissing you," True muttered, pulling her firmly back into his embrace. He lifted a hand to her face and trailed a thumb along the straight, set line of her jaw. Her skin was as soft as it looked, and kissing each freckle could keep a man busy for a long, long time. "You taste as grown-up as you look, Slim."

She glared at him. "Is that your idea of a compliment?"

In response, he kissed her again. Against her lips, he murmured, "How about if I say you taste like sin, but feel like a blessing?"

She shivered, but didn't try to break away. "I don't know why you're doing this."

"Because I want to. I want you."

She held off another kiss. "You're acting like a crazy fool."

He stepped back. "So you don't want me to kiss you?"

She couldn't tell him that. Her mouth opened. True saw muscles work in her throat as she tried to speak. But not a sound escaped. He laughed in triumph and, predictably, that made her mad.

Flouncing away, she said, "You've got a warped sense of humor."

"You've always known that. In fact, you know pretty much everything about me. Which is just one of the reasons why it makes sense for us to get married."

She paced the length of the room and back. "Don't be an idiot. I've been gone for years. I've changed. You've changed."

He studied her slender but undeniably female form for a long, measured moment. "I sort of like the changes in you."

Her hands clenched into fists at her sides. "What an insultingly chauvinistic and macho remark. Are you saying that if I was still skinny and flat-chested, you wouldn't be interested?"

True considered that for a moment, then shook his head. "I don't think I'd care. You'd still be you."

"Yeah, sure."

"Well, I'm not going to stand here and say I wish you were ugly."

Paige's eyes narrowed. "You used to think I was ugly."

"I did not. I just didn't see you as a girl."

"Gee, thanks."

"Until we were grown, I'm not sure I even knew you were a girl."

She snorted. "That makes me feel so much better."

"Damn it, Paige. Why does anything I neglected to notice or mention in my callow youth matter? I'm asking you to marry me now."

She started to say something, then shook her head and held up a hand to ward him off when he started to come closer. "Just stay there, True. I don't want you kissing me again."

Grinning, he ignored her instructions. "Why's that?" he said, advancing on her.

"Because you make me—"

"Crazy?" he suggested with a devilish grin.

"No." He could read the lie in her eyes.

He took hold of her shoulders and brought her close once more. Idly, he noted that she was taller than he remembered. He had always thought of her as such a little girl. But she matched him well, her head tucking just under his chin as he hugged her. "I want to marry you, Paige."

She held herself stiff in his arms. "So we see each other at the feed store this morning, sit down for a piece of pie tonight and all of a sudden you're in the throes of passion for me. I don't buy it, True."

"It's not exactly passion."

She stirred, but didn't draw away to look up at him.

"We're right for each other," True continued. "We want the same things out of life."

Silent for a moment, when she finally spoke, her

voice wasn't quite steady. "What is it you think I want?"

"To live and work here, where our families have always lived and worked."

She didn't reply.

"And I suppose..." True's confidence slipped a bit, but he blundered on. "At the risk of sounding like a chauvinistic jerk again, I'm supposing that you would like what most women want. A family. Babies."

That made her draw away, and even in the dim light of the lamps and the fire, True could see her face was flushed. "Yes," she admitted after a long pause. "I do want children. Something you already have."

"So you know I'm capable of reproducing."

She shot him a look sharp as a spur. "You talk about yourself like a prize bull."

"Might as well be practical about matters. You want children. I could give them to you."

"Give them to me?" she repeated, aghast. "That's how you think of having children? You *give* them to the woman? What in the world—"

"That didn't come out the way I intended," True protested. "I meant to say I would love to have more children before I get any older."

"You're only thirty-three, True. That's not seventy-three."

"It's not twenty-three, either." He cleared his throat. "Neither is thirty-one the same as twenty-one."

Her eyes flashed at the mention of her own age.

"So now you're saying I'm getting older every day, too, and I'd better grab this chance while I can. You think you're my last salvation before spinsterhood?"

He exhaled in frustration, wondering how this conversation got so out of control. "I'm sure you've had a lot of chances to get married."

That appeared to cool her temper a degree or two, even as it raised her chin. "Yes, if you must know, there have been men in my life."

For some reason, that claim clenched True's stomach. "Men?" he repeated.

"A few." She made a great show of playing with the sparkly bracelet on her left wrist. The jewels looked like diamonds, quite a lot of them. "A few generous men."

True figured a bracelet like that would cost more head of beef than he would be able to spare in the near future. And despite the comfortable life Paige had enjoyed as Rex McMullen's daughter, her obvious pleasure in the bauble surprised him. "I never thought of you as the mercenary type."

"Well, not every man I've dated has bestowed such wonderful gifts. I didn't confine myself only to rich men."

The knot in his gut hardened.

"A poor but sincere man can be just as appealing," she added, slanting a look at him again. "I've done some comparison shopping."

"I never would have pegged you as a social butterfly, either."

"Just shows you don't know everything about me."

His eyes narrowed. "I know you'll be faithful after we're married."

"You sound awfully confident."

"You may have picked up a few bad habits out in California." He flicked a glance toward the bracelet again. "But you're a loyal person at heart, once you've made a commitment. You learned that at your father's knee. You'd sooner sell your soul than betray your word or break a marriage vow."

She threw up her hands with a sound of disgust. "Would you please stop this marriage nonsense? I'm not marrying you."

"You want me to beg?"

"Of course not."

But he was already going down on bended knee before her. "I'll do this the old-fashioned way. Say you'll marry me, and tomorrow I'll ask Rex for your hand."

Paige blinked down at him. "This is too much. You really are making a fool of yourself."

"If you want to save my pride, then say yes."

She reached for his hands, but only to haul him to his feet. All the while she was staring at him with a stunned expression. "You're serious about this, aren't you?"

"I want to marry you."

"You're insane."

"I'm lonely."

"You could take care of that problem with someone else," she retorted, sarcasm heavy. "You've got women lined up, ready to ease your loneliness. Propose to one of them."

"I don't want anyone but you."

"You can stop that 'only you' nonsense right now." She rolled her eyes. "You've already admitted this isn't passionate love you're offering."

He raked a hand through his hair, searching for the right words to explain why he wanted to marry her. "I like being a husband, Paige. I'm good at it."

She was silent, her eyes big and solemn.

"I like being married. Coming home to the same person. Being committed. Settled. Working together." He smiled. "That's when it's good, Paige, when you're comfortable with someone, at ease, at home with them."

"Like with a loyal old dog," she suggested.

He gave her a steady look. "That's not what I mean at all. I'm talking about deep feelings. Friendship."

"Friends don't usually make babies together."

"Believe me, once a couple deals with a colicky baby a few times in the middle of the night, they're lucky if friendship is all they have left."

"Speaking of kids," Paige said, cutting another glance at him. "What about yours? Exactly how were you going to explain this sudden urge to marry someone they don't know?"

"The twins know you."

"I've met them two or three times, years ago. They don't know me at all."

He waved off her concern. "Ever since they were in diapers, Aunt Helen has been giving them blow-by-blow accounts of all the trouble you and I caused around these two ranches. You're already a member of the family."

"That's not the same as introducing me as your wife-to-be and their potential stepmother."

Hope stirred inside him. "Does that mean you're considering my proposal seriously now?"

"No," she protested, putting a hand to her forehead. "I mean..." She groaned. "I don't know what I mean."

"Maybe you mean maybe."

Her brow knit in confusion. "What?"

He grinned. "*Maybe* you'll marry me?" Instead of waiting for her answer, True kissed her again. Lightly at first, but with increasing power.

And when it ended, he felt decidedly unsteady. He pushed a hand through the rusty-gold curls that brushed her shoulder. "Tell me maybe," he urged her. "Maybe?"

She pushed him away, sputtering.

But she didn't say no. And True knew he had her. He kissed her again, left her with the promise that he would get the answer he wanted from her soon.

Remembering that promise while the morning came to life across the snow-frosted land, True leaned over and patted Goldie's neck. The big horse stirred restlessly beneath him before he urged her forward, through a shallow ford in the icy creek.

On the other side, on McMullen land, True gave Goldie her head. He was suddenly eager to get matters settled with Paige. She was going to marry him. Soon.

"Can I have the jelly or are you claiming it as your own?"

Paige looked at her father across the breakfast table, and gradually realized what he was saying. Sheepishly, she handed him the jar of grape jelly she had been holding for more than a few moments. "Sorry."

Rex gave her a long look from beneath his graying eyebrows. "What's got you so serious, daughter?"

She considered telling him about True's ridiculous proposal, but thought better of it. Regaining his strength and learning to live with his diminished abilities was all her father needed to be thinking about. Besides, Tillie was standing by the stove, her ear for gossip cocked in the table's direction. The only person Paige could possibly discuss True with was her best friend, Kathryn Nolan. Or most likely, it was best not to tell anyone about True's proposal. He was probably regretting every word he had said. Every look. Every kiss...

Paige pushed her plate away, wishing it was as easy to push away thoughts of True's kisses. To her father, she said, "I'm just thinking about what I need to do today. The books are in terrible shape, and I've got to get them straightened out before we know exactly where things stand."

Rex frowned. "I'm sorry you've come home to a mess."

Getting up, Paige dropped a kiss on his forehead before carrying her breakfast plate to the sink. "Don't you go worrying about anything. That foreman of yours just got behind in his bookkeeping. I'll catch it up."

Still looking concerned, Rex said, "Shouldn't Jarrett have checked up on the bookkeeping?"

Paige wanted to say that there were a great many things both her younger brother and the ranch foreman should have done while Rex was in the hospital struggling for his life. But that would only upset him. "Dad, you know I'm the one who inherited your head for figures. Jarrett will probably be a brilliant surgeon someday, but he can't add two and two."

Tillie spoke up then. "Seems to me that ever since your brother broke his engagement last August, he hasn't been able to do much of anything."

Over Rex's head, Paige sent the older woman a quelling glance. "I think Jarrett is doing just fine, considering all that's been going on." She patted her father on his shoulder. "Don't listen to Tillie."

Tillie sniffed, but Rex looked reassured. In fact, he looked particularly good this morning. Since coming home a week ago, this was the first time he had felt like having breakfast with them. Or, as Tillie had insisted, it was the first time Paige had stopped coddling him and encouraged him to have breakfast somewhere other than bed. His right side, weakened by the stroke, was improving little by little, with physical therapy. The doctor was encouraging normalcy. However, Paige didn't want to undo any positive steps by upsetting her father over ranch concerns she believed she could handle herself. Just going over unpaid bills with him yesterday afternoon had worn him out.

"I'm headed to the office." Paige gave her father a last smile and reminded him his physical therapist was supposed to visit midmorning. On the way out the door, she plucked her coat from the row of pegs. Tillie followed her onto the tiny kitchen porch.

"You'll catch your death," Paige advised in perfect mimicry of the warning Tillie issued every time the mercury dipped below forty.

"It isn't that cold," the woman retorted. "And I have something to say to you."

Sighing, Paige murmured, "I don't suppose it would matter to you that I don't want to hear a lecture?"

Tillie ignored her. "You ought not to keep so much of the ranch business from your father."

Paige set her jaw.

"Don't take that hard look with me," Tillie warned. "Your father may be down, but he's far from out. You can't cut him out of things around here."

"I would never do that."

"Then tell him what's happening. Be honest. Keep him involved."

With a heavy sigh, Paige rubbed at the headache that was gathering at her temples. "What should I tell him, Tillie? That bookings are down for the spring season. That Jarrett flunked half his classes last semester. Or that Dad's trusted foreman, Paul Parkins, just let the bills sit, but managed to cut himself a generous bonus while he was doing the payroll last month?"

Tillie's faded blue eyes nearly left their sockets. "I told your father months ago that Paul was up to something."

Paige already regretted speaking so frankly with the woman, especially about the foreman. "Please don't mention this to Dad or anyone else. It was yesterday afternoon before I figured out what Paul has done, and I'm going to speak to him today. Maybe there's a perfectly good reason for his writing himself a big check.''

"I think you ought to tell your father."

"I'll tell Dad when I know the whole story."

Drawing her sweater tight against the cold, Tillie shook her head. "I know you've come back to run things, Paige, but you can't take everything away from your father."

"Believe me, I want to run the ranch *with* him, not on my own. I'll be happier than anyone when he's strong enough to get back to work."

"Are you going to decide that for him, or let him test his strength for himself? He's not an invalid. But he could become one if you treat him that way."

Paige turned on her heel and started down the snowy steps. "I don't want to talk about this right now, okay? I have work to do."

"Something to do with True Whitman?"

Wondering if the woman had been listening at the doorway of the study last night, Paige tossed a sharp look over her shoulder. "What are you talking about?"

Tillie pointed toward the nearby outbuilding that matched the ranch house in stucco and brick construction and architectural design. "Isn't that True riding around the corner of the office?"

"Damn," Paige muttered, recognizing the unmistakable figure sitting tall in the saddle on a beautiful palomino.

"Ladies do not swear," Tillie informed her.

But Paige ignored the admonition as she crunched through the snow toward the office. She would just as soon not see True right now. Not with the memory of his kisses so clear and so strong. But she was no coward, and she couldn't avoid him forever.

She wished she could silence the voice inside her that suggested that avoiding True Whitman was last on her list of things she wanted to do with him.

As for all those things she did want to do with him—they made her heart race and her face burn. She hoped to heaven True couldn't tell what she was thinking.

Thinking of how hard Tillie had worked to make her a lady, Paige prayed to the Lord above to save her from herself, even as she raised her hand in greeting to the only man with whom she had ever wanted to sin.

Chapter Three

True stopped the horse and swung to the ground. Cheeks red, his breath fogging in the cold morning air, he was the very picture of healthy, vital masculinity. He waved at Tillie, declined the invitation to breakfast she called out and turned to Paige when the older woman had gone back into the house. "Been thinking about my proposal, Slim?"

Ignoring his unsettling smile and flippant question, she stroked the big horse's soft nose. "I wish you'd stop calling me that silly nickname."

"Some women would kill to have the figure for it."

Paige tried not to react to the appreciative gaze he slid over her. She was glad she had decided to wear presentable jeans and put on a little makeup this morning. But she wasn't about to let him turn her head today as he had last night. She patted the horse again and changed the subject. "This pretty girl has to be Golden Chance's daughter," she said, referring to a favorite mount of True's from long ago.

Nodding, he told Paige the horse's name with a proud smile.

"Goldie, you are beautiful," Paige crooned to the animal.

"She's got a daughter you'd love to ride."

"Golden Chance's daughter has a daughter." Paige sighed. "I've been away from home a long time."

"I bet you'll be here to see the granddaughter's granddaughter."

"You're right," she agreed. "I'll be right here on my ranch while you're on yours."

His smile slipped a notch. "Is that my answer?"

The sensible thing would be to tell him right now that his proposal was ridiculous and insulting. That she wasn't interested in marrying a man who didn't love her. A man who was suggesting they build a marriage on the leftover memories of a childhood friendship. A man who was probably looking for a mother for his children as much as a companion for life. The idea was preposterous and impossible.

But the man was True.

Because she was afraid the half-buried dreams of her heart would shine in her eyes, Paige turned toward the office and left True to tether Goldie. Paige knew he would follow her, but by the time she faced him again, she hoped to have her emotions and her expression under control.

Inside the spacious but functional office, she tossed

her coat onto a nearby rack, checked the answering machine and turned on the computer. When spring and the first of the Double M's guests arrived, seasonal employees would be bustling about the office. The large and comfortably appointed guest lounge that adjoined the office would be open and busy, as well. But until then, the lounge was closed off and quiet, and Paige didn't see any signs that the ranch foreman had been in the office this morning, either. She hoped he was directing some winter work on one of the barns, as she had asked him to do yesterday, but she had less and less confidence that the man was doing much at all. She wasn't looking forward to her confrontation with him.

It would help if True would take his distracting self out of here. Instead, he was making himself at home, ditching his hat and coat and starting up the coffeemaker.

Taking a seat at the desk, she protested, "If you don't mind, I have work to do."

Unconcerned, he settled himself on the desk corner. "There's nothing more important than my proposal."

Paige tried to dodge him, but True trapped her, wedging one cowboy boot against the rollers on her chair and leaning forward with both hands on the chair arms, his steel-muscled arms locked on either side of her.

She tried looking away, not an easy task given the proximity of his handsome face and broad shoulders and the intensity of his gaze. She failed, finally, and had to face him.

His voice was a soft, deep drawl. "Don't say you

don't want to marry me, Paige. I can see the truth in your eyes.''

She decided to go for honesty. A least partially. "Okay," she admitted. "The idea of marrying you isn't completely distasteful.''

He smirked. "With sweet talk like that, I could get a swelled head.''

"Don't joke, True. This is too serious.''

His brilliant smile faded, and he leaned back, releasing her chair from his iron grip. "Of course it's serious.''

"But you're joking around. It's clear you acted on impulse last night. I figured you'd come to your senses after a good night's sleep, but since you haven't, I have to do it for you. I'm not going to hold you to this proposal.''

"What does that mean?''

"Once you've had time to think about this, you'll realize what a mistake you've made. I don't want this standing between us once that happens. Let's just forget it.''

His features hardened. "The proposal stands. And, as you should know, I am not an impulsive man.''

"Last night was an exception.''

"I don't take marriage lightly. I want to marry you.''

He said he could look at her and see the truth in her eyes, but she wondered if he could possibly see how his words twisted her insides. Once upon a time, in a girlhood dream, she had yearned to hear these words from him. But in her dream, his face and his voice had been softened by love, not edged in simple practicality.

She sat back, hands clenched on her jeans-clad thighs. "Tell me why, True. What's the real reason you're pushing this harebrained scheme? Are you trying to get hold of the Double M? I know that was a dream of your grandfather's."

He burst out laughing. "Give me a break. If I wanted this ranch, I'd make an up-front offer for it."

"But you can't afford it. Marrying me might be the only way you'll ever own this land."

With a quickness belying his size, True came to his feet. Hands braced on either side of his hips, he glared at her with blue eyes whose coldness rivaled the icicles hanging from the window frame outside. "If you were a man, I might just punch you for that."

Paige had never once been afraid of True, but her heart picked up a beat.

"Do you think I'd do something so low?" he demanded.

Of course she didn't. No matter how long she had been out of touch with this man, she knew him to be as honest as a day's work in the branding pen. She put out her hand. "I'm sorry, True. I know you better than to think you'd do something like that."

He ignored her outstretched hand. The muscles worked in his jaw, a sure sign of temper in this controlled man.

"I'm sorry," she repeated. "There's no need to get all bent out of shape."

"Just tell me one thing," he demanded. "What would I want with a *dude* ranch, anyway?"

She caught the teasing edge in his voice. "You rat." She wadded a convenient piece of paper and threw it at his head.

Laughing, he ducked and pulled her up out of the chair.

She said, "Any time you want to compare bottom lines, neighbor, I'll put our dudes up against your beef."

"Comparing bottom lines sounds interesting."

And just like that, the atmosphere between them went from teasing to intense. One minute they were laughing. Then True was looking at her. And she was again trying not to look at him. The question he had put forth last night, the proposal, lay between them like a living creature. But that wasn't all. If that had been all, Paige might have been able to breathe.

Along with the unspoken proposal came a zigzag-ging current of awareness. Tangibly, completely sex-ual, the feeling was raw, crystallized power. Paige felt they were drawing all the energy from the room. She expected the lights to dim, the computer to wink off. And that was with only their hands touching. She could imagine…no, she *would* not allow herself to imagine the two of them touching in a more intimate manner.

True managed to speak first. "It could be good, Paige."

She wondered what "it" he was referring to.

He demonstrated his ability to read her mind. "Not just the sex, though I have a feeling that would be spectacular."

Paige's heartbeat, unsteady for several minutes now, was tripping along at an erratic, lightning speed.

True continued, "We practically grew up in the same playpen. Surely knowing each other that well gives us an edge. We don't have to go through all that courting nonsense, all that figuring each other out. That's what I detest about dating. We don't need that, Paige. We already understand each other."

She bit back a protest. He thought they knew each other in and out. But he didn't know her. By the time she had left here at nineteen, he had been woefully out of step with her deepest feelings.

"You have to agree with me," he murmured. "Our backgrounds are so similar that we can't help but get along. Hell, we always got along."

Still she said nothing. She was afraid if she started talking she'd reveal just how in love with him she had been when he had married Marcie. At their wedding, she had danced with him with tears in her eyes, but she knew True had never figured out the depth of her feelings for him.

A few days before the wedding, when Paige realized he was truly going to marry someone else, they had quarreled about Marcie. He had thought Paige's wedding day tears stemmed from that disagreement. With brotherly tenderness, he had patted her on the shoulder and forgave her for suggesting Marcie would make an unsuitable rancher's wife. He didn't acknowledge that Paige had offered herself as a willing candidate for the position Marcie was taking. He had left Paige standing alone while he returned to his bride.

Paige had run. First to home, where she had been unable to hide her tears or the reason for them from Tillie. The older woman had helped Paige convince Rex to send her to a new college in Dallas. Then Paige moved on to a series of interesting jobs, all far from here. She had kept going, trying not to look over her shoulder. She had met those men she had bragged about to True last night. And not a dozen of their kisses had affected her as did one glance from this tall Texan.

But she wasn't still in love with him. What she felt was leftover yearning, a part of her childhood she hadn't let go.

Or was it?

True put his hand on her shoulder. Through her thin sweater, she felt the warmth and strength of his fingers. In his eyes she saw the steady, solemn honesty of the man at whose side she had grown up. In his kiss last night, she had tasted the promise of passion. He didn't love her, but he was True, and he was offering her half of her dream.

Was it enough?

"Paige?" True prompted. "You know how good this could be, don't you?"

"Maybe," she said, her voice not quite steady.

Obviously sensing her weakening state, he moved closer. "I need you, Paige. I need your support, your comfort, your friendship."

She hesitated, then asked the question most on her mind. "Is that what you had with Marcie?"

If mention of his first wife caused True pain, he didn't show it. Instead, his gaze remained intent on

Paige's as he answered, "Marcie and me were so young. Too young, I see now. We thought every problem could be solved because we were crazy about each other."

"Didn't that help?"

He hesitated only a second. "Maybe."

Filled with sudden, shameful jealousy, Paige turned from him. "I don't understand," she whispered. "If you loved her, and you were happy, how can you consider marriage to someone you don't love?"

"But I do love you, Paige."

His quiet words brought her around to face him again.

"I've loved you my whole life," he said. "For nearly twenty years, you were my best friend. There was never anyone else like you. Never will be, either."

But she knew the sort of love he referred to. "I'm like a sister, you mean."

He took a step forward. "That's past. That's when we were kids. I can assure you there's nothing brotherly in the thoughts I'm having about you now. If I felt that way, I could never ask you to marry me."

Her mouth went dry at the husky undertone in his voice.

"If you'd like me to prove it," he whispered, coming toward her.

She retreated behind her desk chair, knowing she would be lost if he touched her right now. "This is what's confusing, True. You talk about friendship and the practicality of us getting married, and then you look at me..." She swallowed. "You kiss me and say you want children and more than…more than just friendship.''

"I want a marriage," he said. "A full, complete marriage. The kind that will keep both of us happy and satisfied. In and out of bed.''

A flush crawled up Paige's neck and into her cheeks. The image of herself sharing a bed with this man was powerful enough to press the air out of her lungs.

True was coming after her again, a determined, hot look in his eyes. "If you're worried about…" He hesitated, a grin just crooking the corners of his mouth. "About *that*. I'm not opposed to a test run.''

Paige didn't realize she was again backing away until she hit the wall behind her. Startled, she let loose a four-letter word that would have earned her an ear-blistering lecture from Tillie.

True's grin deepened. "You seem nervous, Slim.''

"You're crowding me," she protested. "Stalking me like a mountain cat. I can't think.''

He pushed the chair that stood between them out of the way. It hit the desk with a clang.

Paige flinched.

True kept coming. "Then don't think. Just say yes and be done with it. I believe you want to.''

Paige halted his advance with a hand against his chest. She wanted to be strong and sensible, not swayed by her scattered emotions. "Stop trying to stampede me, True Whitman. Even if I wanted to marry you, I couldn't now. I just came home to run this ranch, to help my father.''

"Your father's going to be back in control soon.''

She shook her head. "He's never going to be the same."

"Things will be different, yes, and I know he's going to love having you here, but he needs a daughter and helper, not a caretaker. You don't have to give him your whole life."

"But I have to take care of things for him," she insisted. "I can't let him down."

"He'll be thrilled when we get married. It'll go a long way toward mending his health."

"You and Tillie think it's going to be so simple for him to pick up the reins again."

Much as Tillie had done, he said, "You have to let him find his own way. You can't do it for him."

"But there's so much to do. So many problems." She again stopped short of confessing the full extent of the Double M's cash flow shortcomings.

"I'm not asking you to turn your back on this ranch." True reached out and touched her face. "I'm just asking you to marry me."

He made something complicated sound far too simple. But Lord, how Paige was tempted. The yearning boiled up inside her as fast as a West Texas dust devil. She wished she didn't want this. She wished this man and his damned proposal didn't feel like the perfect end to a long journey.

Since leaving home, she had been looking for the right place, the right job, the right man. No house by the ocean had satisfied her like this slice of Texas. No cushy job had felt as good as the memory of working alongside her father here on the ranch. No other man was True. She was home on the ranch.

Now True was offering her his hand. Shouldn't she complete the picture?

The risks were awesome. The potential for heartbreak was very real.

But this could also be her one chance at happiness. Her turn on the bronco-busting ride called fortune. Did she dare?

She looked at True, and perhaps he saw her answer before it was fully formed in her mind. A smile broke across his face, a smile that was a trifle too smug, but altogether charming, as were all of True's smiles. Bracing one hand on either side of her, he leaned forward and kissed her. A gentle kiss, as full of promise as his whispered, "I swear I'll make you happy, Slim. I'll look after you, keep you safe."

Those words struck Paige as particularly old-fashioned. Being looked after was hardly the benefit she sought from this marriage. She could look after herself. But she didn't dwell on that. Concentrating on True's next kiss was much more interesting.

He pressed her against the wall. Her arms crept round his neck. He was so big, the muscles of his chest and arms solid and strong. Somehow his hands found their way to her hips and slipped down, until they cupped her bottom. With no apparent effort, he lifted her up. Her legs parted. And his pelvis pushed hard against hers.

Hard was the operative word, Paige thought. The ridge of flesh beneath his zipper became more distinct with each press of his body. In response, her own body was going soft and pliant. Her head was spinning. She had the feeling that if she moved, if she

gave the word, True would have her. Right here.
Right now. Right up against the wall.

"We shouldn't," she murmured, panicking.

He kissed the pulse beating in the hollow of her
throat. "Why not?"

"It's crazy."

True leaned back to study her with eyes that were
sleepier, sexier, bluer than usual. "Aren't engaged
couples allowed to be a little crazy? I think it's okay.
As long as we do it together."

Her protest was a feeble squeak cut off by another
kiss. She went with this kiss, let it bamboozle her.

Until a throat was cleared.

Until someone laughed.

Knowing that laugh as well as she knew her own,
Paige peeked over True's shoulder. Tillie and her father were just inside the door. Rex was in the wheelchair he used to negotiate long distances. Tillie was
behind him. They both looked...delighted? No, that
couldn't be right.

As a surge of embarrassed heat streaked through
her, Paige decided she was losing her mind.

True, damn him, glanced at the two intruders and
just laughed. As if he was used to being caught with
a woman backed into a corner.

Paige pushed at him, but he held on. To Rex, he
said, "We didn't intend to tell you this way—"

"No," Paige interrupted, shoving harder at him.
"We don't intend—"

"We're getting married," True announced.

And for a moment, the changes illness had brought

to Rex McMullen's face cleared away. He beamed. Positively beamed.

Paige got away from True and started toward him. "Dad, please…"

"I knew it," he said. "I knew last night something was happening between you two. Before I went to sleep, I told myself this was it. This was why I lived when all those doctors thought I'd die."

Shock stopped Paige in her tracks. "Dad, what are you saying?"

"That I'm happy," Rex replied. "Very, very happy. The Double M and the Circle W ranches, joined at last. After four generations as neighbors, I'd say it's about time!"

Unemotional, critical Tillie was wiping tears from her cheeks. "I knew it, too. I had a feeling. I just didn't know it would happen this quick."

True reached Paige's side again, took her hand. "We're getting married as soon as we can."

Paige started to protest, then stopped. Why was she fighting this? She glanced from beaming face to beaming face, realizing nobody else had the slightest misgiving about this marriage.

She looked at True. She took a deep breath. And held it. Her pulse was hammering just like the first time she had tried her hand at breaking a horse. If she remembered correctly, True had gotten her into that mess, too. He had laughed when she landed on her butt in the dirt. Then he had put out his hand, hauled her up and pushed her back on the horse for another try. With True, she had always taken chances.

So why not gamble big?

Paige let out her breath. She squeezed True's hand, her gaze unwavering. "I guess you're right. We're getting married."

"You've lost your mind. You can't marry Paige a week from Sunday."

Of all the reactions True had imagined from his Aunt Helen, her horrified protest was last on the list. When he arrived home from the impromptu engagement announcement at the Double M, the twins were at school and his aunt had gone into town for a visit with a cousin and some shopping. It was almost three o'clock before Helen came home and True delivered his news. Instead of the congratulations he expected, she harangued him for nearly ten minutes without allowing for interruption.

"Dadblastit," he fumed when she at last paused for breath. "I thought you wanted me to get married."

"Of course I do."

"Then what's wrong?"

She wrenched open the refrigerator door and impatiently began unloading grocery sacks. "You can't just decide to do a thing like this."

Stepping forward to help her with the food, he demanded, "Did you or did you not meet your 'dear Jake' one night and run off with him the next?"

"That was different. I was seventeen years old, and love at first sight had robbed me of the little sense I possessed."

"And you dare fuss at me?"

"I didn't have two children to think of."

"I am thinking of them. They need a mother."

"So you just decided to go out and get one for them?"

"I finally looked in the right place for the right woman. Yesterday, that's exactly what you told me to do."

Aunt Helen banged the refrigerator closed. "Don't blame this on me."

"I'm not. I made up my mind this was what I wanted, and I did it."

"You made up your mind?" Helen echoed, rolling her eyes. "I swear to the Lord above, I always knew you had tunnel vision about some things, but this takes the prize."

"I beg your pardon?"

"You heard me," she retorted. "All of your life you've gone full speed ahead, damn the consequences. If you set your mind on something, then— bam!—you go for it without stopping to think or to look in either direction."

Elaborately polite, True said, "Excuse me, I thought I was just being determined and focused and all the other things you taught me to be."

Helen opened and closed cabinet doors with undue force. "Determination and focus works just fine when you're rebuilding a ranch. It's another matter entirely to be so single-minded when it comes to dealing with people and their feelings. When your mind is made up about something, there's hell to pay to anyone who gets in your way."

"It's nice to know you hold me in such high regard."

"I regard you just fine, except when you get one of these damn fool notions in your head."

"I don't believe marrying an intelligent, lovely woman, someone I've known all my life, can be termed a damn fool notion." True slammed a cabinet door of his own, just for emphasis.

Fuzzy white curls stuck out on either side of Helen's plump, flushed face like exclamation points. She took a deep breath. "It isn't the woman I'm objecting to."

With heavy sarcasm, True said, "I'm sure Paige will be pleased to know you approve of her."

"Since Paige McMullen spent almost as much time on this ranch as she did at home, I'd be as much to blame as anyone if she hadn't turned out right." Helen paused for just a moment, as if considering her words carefully. "If you want to know the truth, me and Tillie hoped you and Paige might get involved."

"Yes, *Tillie* seemed pleased." His inflection chastised his aunt for not sharing her friend's reaction to the upcoming marriage.

"I imagine so. Tillie always has been a romantic fool."

"Tillie's romantic?" True couldn't imagine anything being further from the truth.

"The kind of romantic only a spinster can be. It's just like her to go all runny-eyed at the idea of you sweeping Paige off her feet."

"Some tears from you wouldn't be unappreciated. If this is what you and Tillie wanted, then what's all the shouting about?"

"It's the haste," Helen snapped. "What's the hurry? Can't you wait a while to get married?"

"Why wait to marry someone I've known forever?"

"Maybe to figure out if you still like each other."

"Of course I still like Paige. I asked her to marry me—"

"But how do you *feel* about her?"

"The way I've always felt."

His aunt's disbelief was palpable. "After all these years apart from her, how can you know how you feel?"

"The only difference I can see is that now she's one damned fine-looking woman."

Helen sniffed. "Just like a man to notice that first."

True shoved a hand through his hair, frustrated that Aunt Helen was throwing a kink into his plans.

"Have you kissed her?"

Her abrupt question took True by surprise. "What does that have to do with anything?"

"If you have to ask, I'm shocked those twins ever got into this world. Now, have you kissed her?"

Though used to his aunt's directness, True shuffled his feet self-consciously. "Of course I've kissed her."

"And how was it?"

"Aunt Helen—"

"Just answer the question, boy. How did you feel?"

Turned on, True wanted to reply. But as close as he was to his plain-talking aunt, he couldn't admit that. It just didn't feel right, admitting to Helen that kissing Paige made him hotter and harder than a branding iron.

Helen, as usual, read his mind. "So that's the way it is. You liked the way Paige looked, did you? Then you kissed her, and you started thinking with your—"

"Aunt Helen," True protested before she could utter another word.

Undeterred, she continued, "It's just like a lonely man to listen to his gonads instead of his brain."

He straightened his shoulders, his irritation with her going from mild to extreme. "I proposed before I kissed Paige."

"Let's give the boy a medal."

A muscle began to jump under True's right eye. "All right, I'll admit I'm attracted to her. Should I have proposed to someone I didn't want to sleep with?"

"How about proposing to someone your children know?"

"They'll love Paige."

"Oh, they'll like her," Helen said, a smug smile on her face. "At least until she tries being a mother. When that happens, those kids, especially Becca, are going to fight like cornered wildcats."

True disagreed. "You're wrong there. They want a mother. And with you leaving—"

"Is that what this is about?" Blue eyes snapping with temper, Helen settled fisted hands on her generous hips. "I'm leaving, so you went out and proposed to the first woman you could find?"

"Of course not."

"Seems that way to me." A look of pure disgust

on her face, Helen glared at him for what seemed like an eternity. Long enough for him to flinch.

Finally, he said, "Paige is not just any woman."

"You're right. She deserves more than what you're offering."

"I'm offering her my name."

Helen's reply was a tart, "She's got a name."

"She wants a family, children, a marriage. All the traditional things that most women want."

Helen blinked. "Paige? Traditional? When did that happen?"

"You're the one who doesn't know her anymore. She's not the tomboy with skinned knees and sun-burned nose who followed me around when we were youngsters."

"I'm confused," Helen said, pretending dismay. "I thought you said Paige hadn't changed—"

True exploded, "All right, that's enough." He stalked across the kitchen toward the stairs. "I thought you would be happy for me. Pleased. Who knew you'd carry on this way?"

"Don't you walk out on me," Helen commanded with the sort of authority True had been obeying for most of his life. "I'm going to say my piece."

Pausing, True took a deep breath and turned. He might as well. She'd follow him if he tried to leave.

"How are you going to tell the children?" Helen demanded.

"Paige is coming over in a little while to spend some time with us."

"Then what?"

"Then we'll see."

Helen shook her head. "And that's your plan?"

"I'll probably give the kids the news after she leaves."

"Wouldn't it be kinder to give the twins and Paige a little more time to get to know one another?"

"Kinder?"

"This is going to be a shock, True. Billy and Becca don't even know that I'm leaving yet. You can't just spring a stepmother on them."

"They can handle it."

"What makes you so sure of that?"

True shifted his weight from foot to foot. "I know my own kids, Aunt Helen."

"And I don't?" After giving him a sharp look, she went over to the window beside the door to the porch.

He tamped down the anger building inside him. Of course she knew Becca and Billy. She had always been part of their lives, and True was fully aware of the sacrifices she had made on their and his behalf. He took a deep breath and released it slowly, telling himself to be calm.

Helen was looking out the window instead of at him. "You're shortsighted, True. You decide to believe one way about people, and that's that. It doesn't matter if it's the truth or not. You don't bother to look deeper until you have to. Not even with your own children."

He had just about had it with her list of his shortcomings. "Just say what you have to say and be done with it, Aunt Helen."

"You don't know Becca and Billy as well as you think."

"You're wrong," True insisted stubbornly. "They're both a lot like me. We're all three impatient. No kind of long, protracted courtship will be good for them, the same as it's not good for me. It's best for Paige and me to marry, to get on with things. Becca and Billy will respond to the security and the settledness of it."

"And if they don't?"

"They will," True insisted. There was no room in his thinking for any other possibility. Paige was going to be a wonderful mother to his children. He couldn't imagine her being otherwise. She was gentle and sweet enough to nurture them the way Marcie had, and practical enough to guide them like Aunt Helen. Paige would be the partner he wanted and needed. "This is going to work."

His aunt glanced at him, looking singularly unconvinced. "Seems to me that you're banking a whole lot on a woman you haven't been around in twelve years."

"I'll bet on Paige. She's always held her own."

Helen's laughter was dry. "She hasn't been around the twins." She nodded out the window. "But they're home from school and Paige is here and has been outside talking to them for a few minutes now."

"Why didn't you say something?" True asked, starting forward.

"Things have been going just fine out there. No blood spilled yet." Helen arched an eyebrow in his direction. "Are you worried or something?"

True rubbed an impatient hand through his hair.

"Tarnation, Aunt Helen, you act like they're little monsters."

"They can be, you know." She looked back outside, gasped and opened the door, shouting the twins' names.

True followed hard on her heels. In the side yard, they found Billy and Becca and Paige.

A very frazzled Paige, sitting in a mud puddle.

Becca and Billy were sprawled alongside her, both looking mighty guilty.

Chapter Four

In Helen's bedroom, Paige stepped out of her muddy, wet jeans. The older woman had given her a bathrobe and dry socks to put on while her jeans were washed and dried. Paige would have preferred to just go home and change, but True had insisted she stay.

Damp and uncomfortable clothes were the least of Paige's worries. Landing on her butt in mud was hardly an auspicious beginning with True's children. They had all been talking just fine before that. Billy, especially, had seemed pleased to meet the "neat Paige" who had done "cool stuff" with his dad when he was a boy. But now Paige had to face them in Helen's bathrobe. Definitely not neat.

A look in the long, old-fashioned mirror confirmed Paige's suspicions that she looked ridiculous. The robe was bright blue with large pink flowers, far too big, and since she had a good five inches on True's aunt, the hem struck her just below the knees. The heavy white socks admittedly warmed her feet but were something less than flattering.

"Just stunning," Paige muttered to her reflection. A knock sounded at the door before she could worry any longer over her appearance.

The door cracked open and True asked, "You decent?"

"After a fashion." Paige curtsied prettily when he stuck his head in the room.

True surveyed her from head to toe and back again, grinning. "That robe never looked better."

She plucked her dirty clothes off the floor and thrust them at him. "Just put these in the washer, will you?"

True led the way from the bedroom through a small sitting room. These rear quarters had been added years ago in order to give Helen some privacy. They featured worn green carpet and faded, flocked wallpaper. "Yucky" was the only word Paige could think of to describe the decor.

A utility room opened off the hall that connected the addition to the kitchen. Paige was pleased to note the washer and dryer looked new. Except for some attractive changes to the big, country kitchen, she found little had been altered about the ranch house, inside or out, since she was a child visiting the Circle W.

Her jeans and sweater were put in the wash, and Paige and True started toward the kitchen. Becca and

Billy, who had changed clothes as well, were seated at the kitchen table, their backs to the hall entry.

Helen was saying, "Just what happened out there?"

"We fell," Becca supplied.

The older woman, carrying two steaming mugs to the table, looked suspicious. "Are you sure—"

"We did fall," Paige said as she preceded True into the room.

Billy and Becca twisted around to look at her. The boy darted a look at his sister. The expression on Becca's plump features was completely unreadable.

"But how?" Helen asked.

"Good question," True added, his tone stern. "You kids care to tell us how Paige wound up in the mud?"

Paige didn't want this to be turned into a problem just because she had been involved. "It was an accident, pure and simple." She went around the table to accept a cup of coffee from Helen.

"Are you sure?" the older woman asked again. Paige noticed her gaze lingered on Becca.

The child was blithely dipping a cookie in her warm drink.

"The kids were playing in mud puddles near the house when I drove up," Paige explained as she took a seat. "This melting snow, on top of the rain we had earlier in the week, has made everything a mess. I remember when I was these kids' age, I couldn't resist a mud puddle, either." Over the rim of his mug, Billy gave her a grin. Paige smiled back. The boy could pass for his father at the same age.

Helen didn't let up. "But how did you end up in the mud, Paige?"

"The kids were playing. I drove up, got out and introduced myself, and when we all started toward the house, Billy splashed through the mud again. Becca tried to catch him, and I tried to get hold of both of them. That's when we all fell." There was nothing mysterious about it, Paige thought, wondering why Helen seemed so skeptical.

"Sounds like just an accident to me," True said.

Helen, however, continued to look unsatisfied as she turned to fill a mug of coffee for herself.

"You should be used to messes," Paige told her. "True and I landed in enough of them."

Billy said, "Did you guys really set the ranch on fire?"

True laughed. "We set the pasture behind the barn on fire. By accident."

Joining them at the table, Helen clucked her disapproval. "I never was so scared. The weather was hot as fire that summer, and the field was so dry it crackled when the wind blew."

"The wind was the problem," Paige said. "It caught the sparks from the little campfire we were trying to build out beyond the barns."

"Why were you building a fire there, anyway?" Becca asked, rolling her eyes.

"Because I was eight and Paige was six," True answered. "We wanted to go camping, but our parents said we were too little to go by ourselves, which we were. So we decided to show them we could."

"And almost burned the place down." Helen gave

both children a firm look. "So don't go getting any ideas from your father and Paige's shenanigans."

Paige chuckled. "I still remember the spanking you gave us that afternoon, Aunt Helen."

"Once I knew you were okay, I tanned your hides." With a sheepish smile and easy familiarity, Helen laid her hand on Paige's arm.

Billy was regarding the older woman with a confused expression. "Are you Paige's aunt, too?"

Paige glanced at Becca and saw the same question mirrored in her face, although the girl was sporting a slight frown, as well.

"She always called me aunt," Helen said.

"It just seemed natural," Paige added. "Even though we're not related at all."

"You were always like family. You still are." True's smile was wide and charming, and Paige warmed to it and him without hesitation. Heat rushed to her cheeks as the two of them exchanged a look that lingered. The man certainly could do wonderful things to her with just a grin.

Tearing her gaze away took some effort. When she did, however, she found herself being studied intently by the little girl on the other side of the table. Paige smiled at Becca, but the child didn't respond in kind.

Instead, Becca got up from the table and came around to stand beside her father. "Daddy, will you ride with us for a while? You promised to teach us some new tricks the next day you weren't busy."

"You've got homework," Helen said.

"But it's Friday," Billy protested. "And we don't have much to do."

Becca looped her arm through True's. Her eyes were big and blue and pleading. "Please, Daddy?"

He glanced at Paige. "How about you, Slim? You were always the best trick rider on these two ranches. I bet you could show these youngsters a thing or two."

"I haven't done anything like that in years. Besides…" Paige plucked at the robe's collar. "I'm hardly dressed for it."

"Does that mean we can't go?" Becca whined.

"Paige is our guest," True said.

Paige was not eager to come off as the spoilsport of the day. "True, I don't mind if you go riding with the kids."

He shook his head. "I thought we could all do something together."

"I'll visit with Helen while my clothes wash and dry."

"We'll wait, too."

"It'll be dark by then," Paige protested. "Please, go."

Though True still hesitated, Becca clapped her approval and flashed Paige a smile.

Score a point for me, Paige thought, wondering why she felt such intense relief.

In moments, Becca had shepherded her brother and father into coats and out the door.

From her seat at the end of the table, Helen murmured, "She's quite a little leader, isn't she?"

Paige blinked. "What?"

"Our Becca. She likes to organize things."

"That'll be to her advantage some day."

"What about your advantage?" With an enigmatic smile, Helen rose to get some more coffee.

There were some undercurrents here to which Paige wasn't sure how to react. Choosing to say nothing rather than the wrong thing, she just held out her mug for a refill.

The older woman sat down once more. "Paige, are you really going to marry him?"

Paige bit her lip at Helen's tone. "So he told you, did he? I wasn't sure if you…well…you didn't act especially welcoming."

"I'm sorry," Helen replied, her regret genuine. "You know I love you, Paige. It's good to see you." Despite the affection of her words, her generous mouth compressed into a tight line.

Paige's spirits fell. With her father and Tillie carrying on as they had, she hadn't expected disapproval from Helen. "You're unhappy about this?"

"I don't think you know what you're getting into."

"Because of the kids?"

"They are rotten little brats. Hellions."

Shocked, Paige choked on her coffee.

True's aunt jumped up and thumped her on the back. "Don't act so stunned," she said between sturdy whacks. "You of all people should know I call 'em as I see 'em."

Once she was sure she wasn't strangling, Paige sputtered, "But they're True's babies."

"Don't get me wrong," the older woman said. "They're my family, and I love 'em both. But they're spoiled and disobedient. And the main reason is their father. He left the disciplining up to Marcie. Then she was gone, and he tried leaving it up to me." Helen eased down into her chair again, her sigh tired. "I haven't done either of them much good."

"I believe you're selling yourself short." Paige patted Helen's work-worn hand. "You raised True and did a fine job."

"I was younger then. I can't do it with these two. Billy's not so bad, though he likes to make mischief. Becca's the real problem. She's a deep one. She hides her feelings. And you can generally trace any trouble her brother gets into back to her."

"Is that why you were trying so hard to find out what happened out in the yard?"

"I know what happened," Helen replied matter-of-factly. "I was watching from the window. Becca tripped Billy, he grabbed hold of her and you got yanked down with both of them."

"But why would she do that?"

"Her teachers say she's causing scenes because she wants attention. She also feels she has to compete with Billy for True's approval. But I'm sure she didn't intend for you to land in the mud puddle. Far as I know, she's got nothing against you." Helen's smile was grim. "At least not yet."

Remembering the long, assessing glance Becca had directed at her, Paige shifted uncomfortably in her seat. "Aunt Helen, if you saw Becca trip Billy, why in the world didn't you say something?"

"Becca'd just deny it. She's quite a liar, and Billy usually backs her up."

Putting a hand to her head, Paige sat back in her

chair and stared at the other woman. "True calls her his little angel."

Helen snorted. "That's the way he wants to see her."

Paige didn't want to believe Helen was right about these kids. Maybe she wasn't. Helen was getting older. She had admitted she couldn't keep up with the twins. Most likely, what they needed was someone with a lighter touch. Helen was a wonderful woman, but she was naturally gruff, a trait that seemed to have worsened over the years. Becca and Billy were probably just rebelling against her old-fashioned child-rearing ideas.

And after all, their mother had died tragically not three years ago. True had lost his wife, had grieved for her. Maybe he had relied on Aunt Helen a little too much during that time, and once he was feeling better, she had taken over the kids so completely that he couldn't get as involved as he would have liked. Paige simply refused to believe he was letting his children run wild. She said as much to Helen.

The woman just laughed. "You know what the parents of their schoolmates call those kids? Becca the Beast and Billy the Kid."

"Parents say that?" Paige was aghast. "How cruel. Does True know?"

Helen hauled herself to her feet. "True thinks it's kind of cute that the kids are so spirited." With a humorless chuckle, she left the room to put Paige's clothes in the dryer.

Sitting perfectly still, Paige stared down at her cooling coffee. No matter what Helen said, she

wouldn't, couldn't, believe all this about Becca and
Billy. She needed to judge them for herself. She certainly couldn't make any assumptions based on the
few minutes she had spent with them this afternoon.

But maybe it would be best if they put the wedding
off a little longer. They could all get to know one
another. She and the children could see how they got
along. She and True could fill in the gaps left by the
past twelve years.

And he could change his mind.

Paige's stomach clenched at the thought. Ever since
last night, she had been expecting True to back out
of this. She had given him every opportunity to do so
this morning in order to save her own pride. If they
put things off, he probably would change his mind.
And when she was so close to having the man she
had always wanted, how could she put up any road-
blocks? Maybe that was selfish. And maybe putting
together a family was what was best for the children,
as True had told her this morning.

"Still going to marry him?"

The question brought Paige's head up. Helen stood
just inside the doorway from the hall. Paige hesitated
only a moment before answering, "Yes."

"So you still love him that much?"

That query sent the blood rushing to her face.

A tender smile gentled the lines on Helen's face.
She came around the table and put an arm around
Paige's shoulders, much as she might have done
twenty years before. "Surely you didn't think I didn't
know. You always loved him. True was the only one
who didn't see that."

Paige shrugged, trying to appear cavalier. "It was a silly, girlish crush."

Helen's expression sharpened. "So you don't love him now?"

"Not like that."

"Umm."

The disbelieving reply set Paige's teeth on edge. "Things are different. We're both going into this very sensibly. We both know what we want."

"And what is that exactly?"

"We want a family," Paige said, impatient at having to explain what she thought would be obvious. "We both have such feelings for our homes, for this land. True wants to build the Circle W up even more. I'm going to do the same with the Double M."

"You are?"

"Of course. That's why I came home in the first place. True knows that. We're a good match, and we both know what we expect from each other. I'm a mature adult now, and—"

"And True is still True."

Paige's eyes narrowed. "What does that mean?"

"Just that you're as blind as my pigheaded, arrogant and selfish nephew."

The criticism of True rankled. "Now see here, Aunt Helen. While he may be stubborn—"

"Oh, he's that and more. Just as you're much more than he thinks, as well." Helen's hearty laughter filled the room. She laughed until her ruddy cheeks were crimson, until she was bent double, until tears streamed down her face.

Paige demanded, "What in the world is so funny?"

Gasping, Helen said, "It's…just…so hilarious. When I think of True…" She went off into gales of laughter again.

"When you think what of True?"

The older woman managed to hold it together long enough to get a sentence out. "When I think of all that True doesn't know about you, I could bust a gut. This is just what he deserves."

"I don't know what you mean by that," Paige retorted.

Through the tears of laughter, Helen's blue eyes twinkled. "Oh, you will. You and True, you've got a hell of a lot of surprises in store for each other."

Twenty minutes later, clad in jeans and sweater still warm from the dryer, Paige climbed to the top railing of a fence down by the barn. True was in the center of the corral, the children riding around him as he called out instructions. With Helen's comments fresh in her mind, Paige half expected the twins to turn and stampede her. To her relief, they both just waved. Just like normal, happy kids, not at all like the devil's spawn Helen had described earlier.

The first purple shadows of a winter twilight were creeping across the ranch. The air was chilly, but Paige was still steaming about Helen's mysterious predictions about her and True getting what they deserved. No matter what Paige had said, the woman had refused to explain what she found so hilarious. Miffed, Paige had been very happy when Helen refused her offers to help with dinner.

True ambled over to the fence and climbed up beside her. "You and Aunt Helen have a good visit?"

Paige started to nod, then decided to be honest. "She's not as pleased about us as Tillie and Dad were."

He dismissed that with a shrug. "She'll get over it. I think the problem is that she and Tillie were all set for some heavy-duty matchmaking. We took all the fun out of it for Aunt Helen. You know how she likes to be in charge."

"I hope you're right," Paige grumbled. "I'd sort of like to have her support."

"Look at it this way. She wants to retire. Now she can do it sooner."

"What do you mean?"

"With you and me married, she can move to that retirement community a month sooner than she planned."

Mouth suddenly dry, Paige said, "I was hoping she might stay on for at least a few weeks."

"Why?"

"For the kids." She cleared her throat. "They're used to her, and I've got a lot of stuff happening over at our place. There's going to be a lot of adjustments."

"Don't worry." True lifted a gloved hand to brush a tendril of hair from her cheek. "Everything will be just fine once we're married and settled down."

"Are you sure?"

He lightly touched her cheek, then bent forward, as if to kiss her.

From the ring, Billy called out, "Dad, look at me."

True and Paige both glanced up in time to see the boy do a somersault dismount from his roan horse.

"Ye-haw!" True stood and twirled his hat.

"That was terrific," Paige said, applauding.

She was rewarded with a smile and a bow from Billy.

"Look at me," Becca yelled. With much aplomb, she mimicked her brother's move. Not quite as smoothly, but with obvious flair.

Paige and True applauded again.

"Watch all we can do," Becca said, mounting her horse again.

She and Billy put on quite a show. They stood in the saddle while galloping around and around. They rode backward. Did running mounts. They whooped and carried on while Paige and True provided admiration and encouragement.

Darkness came too soon, True thought. He liked sitting beside Paige and watching Billy and Becca perform. He enjoyed the sound of Paige's laughter mixing with his children's. He relished sharing this simple moment of togetherness with her.

The camaraderie continued in the barn, where Paige's skill at grooming the horses was appreciated by both twins. She talked just right to their mounts, low and soothing, the way True had taught Becca and Billy to speak to their horses. She scored lots of points with Becca by being especially solicitous of Poppy. The chestnut mare, due to give birth in early spring, was a special pet of his daughter's. True wasn't looking forward to telling her that he already had a buyer lined up for the foal.

Paige seemed to know instinctively what note to strike with the kids. She was direct and honest. With none of the phony, easy-to-see-through, manufactured interest of the few other women True had brought around the youngsters.

Dinner was just as nice. Billy, who could be a pest, was on his best behavior. Becca put on a display of her finest table manners. Paige listened, really listened, to several long and tedious stories about school and camp.

Across the table, True kept looking at Aunt Helen. He hoped she was getting his messages. *See how good this is. See how they like Paige. See how she fits in.*

The older woman wore a half smile that True could only call gleeful. What was that about?

Whatever it was made Paige uncomfortable. Every time she looked at Helen, she frowned and glanced around the table, studying the children.

Taking herself off to her rooms right after dinner, Helen left the dinner dishes to the rest of them. Billy actually volunteered to help Paige, who insisted on cleaning up. Since more than two weren't necessary for loading the dishwasher, Becca simply perched on a stool beside the counter, talked and pointed out where to find supplies and store the pots and pans Paige and Billy washed by hand.

In the family room area of the big country kitchen, True kicked back in his recliner and savored the sounds of family life. This was it, he thought. This was what he wanted.

Having been challenged by Billy, Paige stayed for a couple of rousing video games. Becca wasn't to be left out, of course. There was much laughter and a lot of fun.

When True walked Paige out to her truck, he pulled her close. "They love you."

"I wouldn't go that far."

"Seriously, they like you a lot."

"I like them."

He leaned forward, capturing her mouth beneath his. In the clear night air that had grown cold, the kiss fanned some definite flames. Yet Paige shivered.

"You're freezing," True murmured. Sliding his hands under her coat, he brought her body flush against his. He could feel the soft fullness of her breasts, the beating of her heart. The moon was so bright, he could see her face clearly. Her eyes shone. Her lips begged to be kissed again. He obliged, lingering over her warm, eager mouth. His body stirred and tightened in response.

"What if the kids look out and see us?" Paige whispered.

"I think they'd approve."

"I'm not sure."

"I'm telling them about the wedding before they go to bed, anyway."

She stiffened. "Shouldn't you wait? Let us do this a few more times? At least wait until morning when they're not worn-out."

"No." He kissed her again for emphasis, then released her and opened her truck door.

"True..." she began.

"It's going to be fine. I know my kids."

She took a deep breath. "All right. Call me in the morning and tell me what they say."

"Sure."

"Or you could call me tonight."

He chuckled. "Not the least bit overanxious, are you?"

"I just want them to be all right with this. This is big stuff, and we're just throwing it at them."

"Leave 'em to me."

"All right," she agreed, drawing in and releasing another deep breath. "Tomorrow afternoon I'm going into town to look at Kathryn's shop for something to wear to the wedding."

Kathryn Nolan, Paige's best friend from college, owned and operated a bridal shop in Amarillo. Kathryn's husband of less than six months was the veterinarian True used.

"You want a wedding dress?" True asked Paige, surprised.

"Sure." She paused. "What did you think I'd want?"

"I hadn't thought about it."

"What are you going to wear?"

He hesitated. "My best suit?"

"Not on your life. I want you in a tuxedo."

"Now come on, Paige."

"No arguments." Her tone was exactly the same as when she was five and she instructed him to teach her to shoot. Neither of them had been supposed to go near a gun without an adult around, but Paige had finally persuaded True to get his BB gun and give her instructions. It had been True's father, not Aunt Helen, who had blistered his behind for that one.

Paige continued firmly, "You have to wear a tuxedo. And I think Billy should have one, too."

"Billy?"

"Becca should have a special dress, as well. This wedding will be important in their lives, too. They should stand up with us."

"Stand up?" True's head was beginning to pound. "What do you mean?"

"Don't you want them to stand with you at the altar?"

"What altar?"

"The altar in front of the living room fireplace at the ranch. Tillie and I were in there planning all afternoon."

He let out a sigh of relief. "For a minute I thought you meant an altar at a church, with guests and cake and punch and..." His words trailed away as he saw her jaw set.

"There are going to be guests."

He groaned. "Who?"

"Family and close friends, like some of the people who have worked at the ranch since I was a kid. Kathryn and Gray—"

"All right, all right." True surrendered, holding up his hand to stop her. "That sounds okay. But a cake and all that stuff?"

"We have to serve them something. Kathryn will want to do all of this for me. Weddings are her business, and even though I've been away, we're still close."

"Isn't she pregnant?"

"The baby's due in about six weeks. Why?"

"Shouldn't she stay home and keep her feet up?"

Laughing, Paige gave him a playful shove. "Don't be silly, True."

"I'm serious."

She just kept laughing. "Why don't you come by Kathryn's shop tomorrow afternoon? You can rent your tux."

"All right," he said, feeling about as enthusiastic as Billy was at bath time.

"Well don't be so happy about it." With an irritated little huff, Paige got in the truck and closed the door.

True opened it. "Don't go off mad."

She sat for a minute, and he could almost hear her counting to ten in her head, before she said, "What kind of wedding was it you were thinking we would have?"

Quite honestly, he had envisioned a trip to a justice of the peace. He had a feeling, however, that he should play it smart and keep that tidbit to himself.

"I hadn't given it much thought," he prevaricated. "I guess that's woman stuff."

Paige rolled her eyes. "Remarks like that are why so many people think Texas men are stuck in the Stone Age. This is *our* wedding."

"Yes, but it's not as if this is my first—" True snapped off the sentence before he could complete it. Not soon enough, however.

Paige's face fell.

The last thing True wanted was to hurt her. "I'm sorry," he said quietly. "That just popped out."

Her gaze met his, steady and straight and very calm. "Why shouldn't it? This isn't your first wedding."

"But it is *our* wedding." He reached out and put his hand over the one she had hooked in a death grip around the steering wheel. "It should be special."

She glanced at his hand, then back up at him. "I promise not to go overboard. Just family and friends for a small wedding at the Double M."

"And I promise not to growl any more about the tux."

Her fingers finally relaxed under his. "Deal."

He gave her a quick kiss. "You drive careful, Slim."

"I'll be waiting for you to call."

Nodding, he closed the door and stood in the cold, watching while she started the engine and drove off. He shoved his hands in his pockets and frowned, realizing that there had been no deal struck between them at all. He had agreed to everything she had wanted in the first place—a wedding at her ranch with him in a tuxedo.

For the first time since he had decided to propose, True felt a prickle of unease.

But keeping his confidence came as natural to him as wearing his own skin. So he straightened his shoulders and went back inside. He wanted to tell his kids the news.

Chapter Five

Heavily pregnant Kathryn Nolan stood in her shop, Blue Heaven Weddings, with brow furrowed, staring at Paige. "I know I've asked you this a couple of dozen times in the past hour, but tell me again why you're marrying True Whitman?"

"Oh, good grief." Paige turned from the many-sided mirror on the dais where she was modeling her sixth impossible wedding dress in an hour. "I'm marrying True because I want to."

"I do wish you would stop relying on that non-answer."

"If you don't like it, then stop asking." Paige scooped up the dress's heavy train and started toward the dressing rooms at the back of the shop. "And show me a dress that I might actually want to wear out in public."

"You two need to stop bickering." Petite, curly haired Devon Long, Kathryn's associate, came across the shop holding out a large, insulated mug. "Kathryn, it's time for you to get off those swollen feet. And here's your water. You're supposed to be drinking at least eight glasses a day."

Groaning, Kathryn cast a look in the direction of the floor. "You mean I still have feet? The only time I see them these days is when I'm lying down."

Devon pointed toward a semicircle of comfortably cushioned deep blue chairs clustered around a low table in the shop's bay window. "Sit down there, put your feet up and let me take care of Paige."

"Good luck with that one," Kathryn muttered, even as she waddled to the chair and sat down with obvious relief. "She thinks she can waltz in here, snap up a dress and plan a wedding for a week from tomorrow. Like we don't have anything else to do."

"I haven't seen any other customers," Paige observed.

Bristling, Kathryn sat up again. "I'll have you know we were run over with business this morning. It is mid-January. Holiday weddings are over and everyone's just beginning to gear up for spring and summer."

"Maybe that's the reason your stock is low. You don't have a dress a sensible, mature woman would want to wear." Paige hiked up her voluminous skirts and turned toward the dressing rooms yet again.

Before Kathryn could shoot back another remark, Devon handed her the bottle of water. "You two need to take it down a notch. Kathryn, all you've done since Paige got here is fuss at her.''

"That's right," Paige said.

Devon then turned on her. "I don't know you very well, Paige, but it seems as if you came in here with a real chip on your shoulder.''

Kathryn shot Paige a triumphant glance. "Just why are you so defensive, anyway? Is it because you knew I was going to ask you a lot of uncomfortable questions about this marriage you're jumping into?''

Paige started to protest, then paused, biting her lip. She should have known better than to try to hide anything from Kathryn. Her friend knew her too well.

They had met just after Paige left Amarillo for college in Dallas. Paige had been nursing a broken heart following True's wedding to Marcie, and Kathryn had just escaped an abusive, foolhardy marriage. The two of them bonded instantly and wound up sharing a small, off-campus apartment. Kathryn, estranged from her family, had often come home to the ranch with Paige for holidays. She had fallen in love with West Texas and moved here upon graduation. Her connection with the McMullens had helped her in establishing her very successful shop.

Though Paige had chosen to go elsewhere to live, she and Kathryn had remained close over the years. Last year, when Paige's younger brother, Jarrett, was engaged to be married, Kathryn had stepped in to coordinate the wedding. The young bride-to-be's stepbrother, Gray Nolan, had become Kathryn's husband, while Jarrett and his intended parted company.

"Well?" Kathryn prompted Paige. "Are you going

to tell me the truth, and the whole truth, about this wedding or what?''

Sighing, Paige let the heavy train and dress skirts fall to the floor. ''It's just what I said, Kathryn. I want to marry True. I always have.''

''You told me you were over him,'' Kathryn accused. ''A long time ago, you said it was probably for the best that he never saw you as anything but a sister.''

''That was when there was no hope of me ever marrying him.''

''So you were lying about your feelings for him?''

''I wasn't lying.'' Suddenly sick of the fussy, too-elaborate veil Kathryn had fitted to her head, Paige yanked it off. ''I'm not in love with True like I was before.''

Brown eyes wide, Devon said, ''So you don't love him?''

Paige looked at her and then at Kathryn. And she said nothing. Not because she was trying to be mysterious, but because she had no idea exactly how to answer that question. For the past thirty-six hours she had scrupulously avoided analyzing her precise feelings for True. Obviously, she had deep feelings for him, else she might have been able to become involved with some other man. Else she wouldn't even consider marrying him.

But if she stopped and thought about whether or not she was truly in love with him, she might become even more frightened than she was now. More frightened than she had been last night when Helen had told her all those awful things about the children, awful things that Tillie and her father, unfortunately, had backed up when she asked them today. But if the question of whether of not she loved True was added to this mix, she might just back out now. Then she would have to spend the second half of her life having the same what-might-have-been thoughts about True as had occupied the first half.

Kathryn leaned her head back in the chair, staring at the ceiling. "Dear Lord, what is this woman doing?"

"I'm getting married," Paige retorted, stiffening her resolve once more. "I want a family, and I want to run the ranch, and marrying True makes wonderful sense for both reasons. He's a kind, decent man who wants to marry me. And my father is just thrilled."

Snapping her gaze back to Paige, Kathryn asked, "Don't tell me you're getting married to please Rex?"

"Of course not. But he is happy. He says that, secretly, this is what he has always wanted." Smiling, Paige thought of the new life she had seen in her father. For the first time since his stroke, she truly believed he was going to be okay. Maybe not his former robust self, but still just fine. "He's already talking about grandchildren."

"How wonderful for him." Kathryn's tone was dry. "And speaking of children…what about True's? How are they taking this?"

"He says they're okay."

Kathryn's eyes narrowed. "He says? Haven't you talked to them yourself?"

Paige told her about her visit with Aunt Helen,

True and the children last night and how well they had gotten along. "He told them we were getting married after I left. But he called to let me know they're doing just fine with it."

"Just fine?" Kathryn set her water aside and linked her hands on her rounded tummy. "Just fine doesn't sound like a ringing endorsement."

Her friend was giving voice to the same sort of doubts Paige had when True called this morning, and she didn't want to hear them. She found herself echoing True's reassurances. "The kids have to have a chance to adjust."

"Some chance, considering the wedding is in a week."

Again, Paige hitched up her skirts. "You know, Kathryn, if you throw this kind of wet blanket on every bride who comes in here, it's a wonder you have any business at all. You really have given in to your need to control everything, haven't you?"

"Don't get mad at me because you left your brain in California."

"Come on, you guys." Devon stepped forward before another barb could be launched. "There's no point to this."

For a moment, the two friends continued to glare at each other. Then a sheepish look appeared on Kathryn's face. Rubbing her stomach, she said, "I'm sorry, Paige. I am a bit fretful these days."

"You have good reason to be." Paige gave a rueful sigh. "I guess I'm a little high-strung myself. Dealing with Dad's stroke, moving, taking over the ranch and now getting married...'' She blew out a breath. ''It's pretty overwhelming.''

Worry crept into Kathryn's green eyes. ''Are you sure this is what you want?''

''We're not starting that again, are we?''

''I'm just concerned,'' Kathryn protested. ''I care about you and don't want you making a mistake.''

Dress swishing about her legs, Paige crossed to Kathryn's chair and gave her friend a reassuring hug. ''I know what I'm doing, so don't worry about me. Just help me put this wedding together.''

Kathryn responded by hugging her back, although she looked as if she wanted to say something more. Paige was glad she held her counsel.

Devon stepped into the breach once more. ''I know the perfect dress for Paige.'' Quick as a flash, she was riffling through a rack marked Sale in the middle of the store.

''Those are all party and bridesmaid dresses.'' Wrinkling her nose, Kathryn started to push herself up once again.

''You stay there,'' Devon ordered. She waved a cream-colored confection toward the dressing room. ''Paige, let's get you into this dress.''

As Paige followed Devon, Kathryn called out, ''That dress is not special enough.''

But it was. Ten minutes later, when Paige emerged from the dressing area and mounted the showroom dais, she already knew this was the most wonderful dress she had ever worn.

The style was a simple A-line. Creamy lace, sprinkled with sequins, covered pale pink silk taffeta. The long, slim-fitting sleeves were sheer lace. The bodice was scooped low enough for just a hint of curves to show. The length was perfect, as well, the full skirt just brushing her ankles.

"Oh, my," Kathryn breathed, staring at Paige. "Oh, my goodness. That is it."

But Devon wasn't through. She found a small spray of silk flowers for Paige's hair, satined and sequined shoes for her feet, and a silk bouquet for her hands.

Kathryn got up, clapping in delight. "You look beautiful, Paige. Absolutely gorgeous."

Paige was too busy staring dreamily at herself in the mirror to pay much attention to what anyone else said. She wouldn't have cared if they said it was awful, because she knew it wasn't.

She had been a skinny cowgirl whose wardrobe consisted mainly of jeans when she left Amarillo at nineteen, but through the years she had learned how to dress to be stylish and still please herself. She liked unpretentious styles and smooth lines. That was what had been wrong with all the other dresses she had tried on today. They had been full of ruffles and flounces and too much detail. But this dress, though not intended as a bridal gown at all, was exactly what she wanted to wear when she got married to True.

Married to True.

The thought made her shiver. Made her smile deepen.

Kathryn came and slipped her arm around Paige's waist. She leaned her dark hair close to Paige's strawberry blond. To their reflection, she murmured, "There's the look, the one I've been searching for since you came in here. The look of an honest-to-goodness bride-to-be.''

Laughing, Paige hugged her. "I'm so happy, Kathryn. You know better than anyone what True has always meant to me."

"He's your first love." Kathryn hugged her again. "There's never anyone who can take your first love's place."

"And I'm marrying him." Paige stepped forward, staring at herself once more. Her pulse fluttered. Her cheeks turned rosy. Her eyes sparkled.

Plain, old-fashioned giddiness assailed her as she pirouetted in front of the mirror.

Kathryn, ever the practical bridal consultant, left the dais and plucked a notepad from a nearby desk. "Let's make a list of everything that has to be done. Devon, you help us."

The three women were deep into a discussion of decorations, flowers and menus when the bell over the shop door jangled. Devon left the other two to check on the customer.

It turned out to be True.

Kathryn immediately jumped in front of Paige. "You get out of here," she ordered True. "You can't see her in this dress. It's terrible, awful bad luck for the groom to see the bride in her gown before the wedding."

"Don't be silly," Paige said, sweeping her aside. "There's nothing to that old wives' tale. I'd like to hear what True has to say."

Grinning at him over her shoulder, she walked the

length of the showroom, executing what she hoped was a model-perfect turn before she walked back.

True said nothing. He just stared.

"Isn't she gorgeous?" Kathryn asked him.

She was, True thought. Paige was about as pretty as anyone he had ever seen. But it wasn't the dress or the shoes or the flowers in her hair. It was the smile on her lips. The glow in her eyes. The color in her cheeks. She looked like…a bride. Which was what she would be one week from tomorrow.

A bride.

His bride.

The same uneasiness that had taken hold of him last night seized him again. It wasn't the marriage, he told himself. He had no doubts there. It was these foolish wedding plans. They didn't need any of this.

As he stood there, searching for something to say, the light faded from Paige's expression. "You don't like the dress?"

He got hold of himself. "It's beautiful. You look wonderful."

Devon chuckled. "Goodness, Paige, we had better get you out of this dress before the poor man faints dead away. He looks pale."

The glance Paige cast his way was uncertain. "You're sure I look okay?"

"Much better than that."

She smiled, appearing relieved. "You can get Kathryn to help you pick out a tux. Black and basic, I think."

True shifted his weight from foot to foot. "About the tuxedo…"

Again Paige looked concerned. "What is it?"

He jerked a thumb toward the door. "I'm kind of in a hurry. The kids are waiting out in the car."

"Well, bring them in," Paige exclaimed. "We can measure Billy for a tux like yours, and there might be a dress here for Becca."

True looked doubtful.

"For heaven's sake." Paige headed purposefully for the door. "I'll go get them."

"Wait a minute," True said, following her. She didn't pause.

Blue Heaven Weddings occupied a converted house, so there was a front porch unlike what might be found on most businesses. It was there True caught up with Paige.

"I'm not sure the kids want to be in the wedding," he told her.

Her eyes widened in alarm. "I thought you said they were okay with this, that they liked me."

"They do like you. I know they do. But being in the wedding…" He shook his head. "They said yes last night, but when we got here a few minutes ago, they said they'd rather not." For which he was eternally grateful. Maybe the kids' reluctance would talk Paige out of this big party. It was turning into a circus. Aunt Helen had been on the telephone with Tillie and assorted friends and relatives all day, making plans and eyeing True with a great deal more amusement than he thought was necessary.

Paige cast a glance toward his truck, where the backs of two dark heads were visible through the rear window. Her mouth set in a firm line. "I want to talk to them."

"Maybe we should just let them be."

"Are we getting married or not?"

He blinked, startled by her challenging tone. "Of course we are."

"Then I'm going to be their stepmother. So I think it should be all right for me to at least talk to them."

"Of course it's all right," True retorted. "It's just that right now—"

"Oh, bother!" With head held high, Paige headed down the steps and across the parking lot in her fancy shoes and lacy dress. She was so quick, she was two strides ahead of True in reaching the truck. There, she rapped smartly on the passenger window.

True saw Becca and Billy look up from their hand-held video game like two startled deer.

"Hi, there," Paige said, smiling as she opened the door.

Suddenly nervous, True cleared his throat. "Kids, Paige wants to talk to you."

Billy looked scared, but Becca seemed perfectly calm as they climbed out of the truck into the mild winter sunshine. His daughter closed the door and lounged against it while her brother stood, glancing from Paige to True and back again.

Paige folded her arms across her middle. "I guess this is all pretty weird for you. Even though I met you both when you were younger, and even though your dad and I have known each other always, you don't know me well at all. But now I'm going to marry your dad, and I imagine that surprised you."

Silence reigned from the twins.

Undeterred, Paige continued, "I'm sure the two of you think your dad and I have lost our minds."

Still no response.

"Here we are, deciding to get married, without asking your opinion. Probably makes you mad."

Frowning, Billy looked at his father. Becca didn't move.

"They're not mad." True reached out and gave Billy's shoulder a reassuring squeeze and sent Becca a smile. He wondered where in the world Paige was headed. "I never said they were mad."

She gave him a withering look. "Of course they're mad. That's probably one of the reasons they don't want to be in the wedding."

"I don't know if that's so," True said, wishing he had called and canceled this tuxedo appointment, or at least left the kids at home. He certainly wasn't going to let Paige badger them about taking part in this wedding. Hell, he didn't want a wedding, never dreamed they would have one. All day today, as the hour approached when he was supposed to meet Paige here, he had been asking himself how he got talked into this without registering more than a cursory protest.

Paige ignored him. "Look," she said to the kids. "If you don't want to be in this wedding, that's just fine with me."

True was surprised.

Becca's eyes narrowed. "It is?"

"Sure," Paige returned. "I just thought it would

be nice for your father to have you guys right beside him.''

Billy slid a glance toward True. ''Do you think it would be nice, Dad?''

What could he do? It would sound mighty strange for him to say he didn't want his children at his side when he got married. On the other hand, if he said he did, they might give in and there went his excuse for lassoing this wedding celebration.

''True?'' Paige prompted.

''Dad?'' Becca added.

He accepted defeat. ''Yeah, it would be nice.''

The twins looked at each other. True knew from experience that they could communicate without a word. They had been doing a lot of that since last night, when he told them he was marrying Paige.

He supposed he had halfway expected them to pitch a fit last night. Becca was usually good at that. In anticipation of an upset, he had asked Aunt Helen to tear herself away from her television set in her room and be with him while he delivered the news. He told himself he wanted his aunt there because he also had to break the news about her leaving, as well. In all honesty, however, when it got right down to telling them about Paige, he had been worried about the reactions he might get. If they objected strenuously, he couldn't marry Paige. At the least they would have to put the wedding off.

But there was no need for worry. Both children had accepted the news calmly. All the news. They were going to miss Aunt Helen. Billy, especially. How much probably wouldn't hit either of them until she was gone. But there had been no scene, no tears, no carrying-on about Paige becoming their stepmother.

Of course, he didn't know what they had said to each other once he closed Becca's bedroom door and left them to talk. He had a feeling Aunt Helen would have liked to have stood out in the hall eavesdropping, but he respected the twins' privacy more than that.

He had fibbed to Paige a little about Becca and Billy's reaction. They had never come right out and said they liked her. He knew they did, of course, because of how well they had behaved around her. Lord knows he had seen them be rude enough to people they disliked, including a few of his dates. He knew also, because...well, they were his kids. And she was Paige. And there wasn't a reason in the world why they shouldn't all get along. But still and all, the most flattering remark made about Paige had been Billy's, "She sure beats the heck out of any of those other ladies you took out, Dad." Becca had concurred.

Given that mild approval, True hadn't been all that surprised when Becca announced they didn't want to participate in the wedding. Since that fit right in with his plans, he didn't waste time trying to convince them.

Paige, still waiting for the twins to say something, said, "I don't want any pressure on you guys about this. The thing I really want is for us all to get along. I want you to be honest with me, and I hope you'll...well, that you'll like me."

"We like you fine," Billy said.

Paige smiled and reached out as if to ruffle the

boy's hair, but seemed to reconsider. A smart move, True thought. Billy hated being treated like a baby.

The boy's responding smile was warm. "I like you fine," he continued. "Everybody says Dad has to marry somebody, so you're as good as—"

"Billy..." True cut in with a gentle rebuke.

Becca rolled her eyes.

Paige's smile slipped.

"What?" Billy asked, looking at everyone in genuine confusion. "What'd I do?"

"It's nothing," Paige assured him. "I appreciate your honesty, and I'm glad you like me."

Becca spoke up. "I'll be in the wedding, if I can pick any dress I want."

Paige cocked her head to the side. "Any dress? Or any suitable dress?"

Momentarily displeased, Becca then shrugged. "Any suitable dress, I guess. Can it be purple?"

"I don't see why not," Paige replied, grinning at her.

The exchange amazed True. Becca was a master at holding people to the very letter of their promises. She was especially adept at getting to wear exactly the clothes she wanted. He had always been happy to let Marcie or Aunt Helen fight it out with her. He wondered why she had acquiesced so painlessly to Paige.

With a heavy sigh, Billy said, "I'll do the wedding, too." He grinned up at True. "For you, Dad."

True patted him on the shoulder. "Thanks, son." Try as he would, he couldn't put any enthusiasm in the words.

Paige didn't seem to notice. She and the kids took off toward the shop. True trailed behind, feeling as if all control over this affair had slipped completely from his grasp.

At the door, he sent Billy and Becca ahead, and held Paige back. "I want to say something to you."

"Something wrong?"

"This wedding," he said firmly. "You promised you'd keep it simple."

"I am."

"Doesn't sound that way to me."

Her eyebrows drew together. "What exactly is it you don't like?"

"Tillie and Helen making plans, calling everyone. Kathryn in there, babbling on about good luck and bad luck. I heard somebody saying something about hors d'oeuvres when I came in. I thought we were having cake."

"Is it a crime to serve a few meatballs?"

"I don't like it." True felt good, exerting his opinion in his usual way. So good that he put a little more force than he intended into his voice. "I don't want a fuss, and by God, I won't have a fuss."

He hadn't expected Paige to roll over and play dead. Neither did he expect her to square her shoulders, look him straight in the eye and say, "And, by God, you don't talk to me that way."

"What?"

Temper flashed in her eyes. "You don't tell me what to do."

"Not even about my own wedding?"

"I am planning the wedding you agreed to last night. Friends, family and a little food."

She had him there. He had stood in the moonlight and looked at her and told her to go right ahead. He should have known better, but he had done it just the same. And True Whitman stood by his word, even when his word was given under the influence of moonlight and kisses.

"All right," he muttered. "Go ahead."

Paige had the audacity to laugh at him. "Don't worry. I was going ahead with it just like it was, no matter what you said."

True ground his teeth.

Just inside the door, Paige turned and hugged him. Her face was all lit up again, like it had been when he came in the shop before. "I'm so excited," she whispered. "So happy."

Kathryn called for her, and she dashed away. But True stood by the door, stunned. Over and over again, he kept seeing her face. So full of happiness. Full of…love?

For the first time True stepped back and took a good look at the ramifications of what they were doing. He had proposed because he wanted a wife and a mother for his children, because he didn't want to court anyone, because Paige seemed to fit all his prerequisite needs. He believed she had accepted for many of the same reasons. But now…

Now she had *the look*. Dewy-eyed and expectant. Not the look of a woman marrying for practicality. Not even a sexual look. No, the expression on Paige's face was different. Softer. Sweeter. Filled with all kinds of hope.

He was in deep water. Over his head.

From the other end of the store, he could hear Kathryn gushing over a flower girl dress for Becca. He kept thinking of Aunt Helen on the phone, of all the relatives, neighbors and friends who had been alerted about the upcoming marriage. As he stood here, someone was probably planning them a party. Rex McMullen was most likely practicing walking with his cane, so that he could escort his daughter to True's side.

True would look like a jerk if he called this off.

He didn't give a damn how he looked.

But he did care about Paige, about what she would feel.

What he kept remembering, clearly, was the Paige who had been nineteen, who had danced with him at his wedding to someone else. Who had cried and said nothing and disappeared. With a clarity he had never possessed before, he realized now what those tears implied. He saw what Marcie had tried to tell him at the time. He saw how deeply Paige cared for him. Obviously, her feelings were still much the same.

Everything that was so simple and so sane was shot to pieces.

He knew now that it wasn't just the wedding that had been bothering him. The problem was what the wedding symbolized. Tender promises and romance. A world of wishes and dreams.

True wanted to turn and walk out. Most of all, he wanted to set the clock back to that moment two days ago when he had run into Paige at the rancher's supply. Not being a superhero, however, he couldn't reverse the rotation of the Earth.

So what he had to do was marry Paige. No hardship there. He still wanted to marry her. He had the same needs, the same goals for the marriage he'd had from the start. But her expectations were different, higher. The consequences of failure, which he hadn't bothered to consider up until now, held the potential for heartbreak. All he could do was hope he could make her happy.

"More than hope," he muttered. "I've got to try."

The spacious living room of the Double M ranch was standing room only. White roses, baby's breath and greenery decked the polished mahogany mantel over the hearth where a small fire burned. The pleasant aroma of wood smoke mingled with the sweet scent of the flowers. Candles glowed in every corner. And an approving sigh rippled through the two dozen or more guests as Paige stepped from the front foyer into the room.

Halfway down the aisle, her father took her arm. He was unsteady with his cane, but determined to give his daughter away. Just feeling him beside her gave Paige strength.

She sought out her brother Jarrett's warm brown eyes. He winked, and she tried to smile.

Kathryn pressed a hand over her heart, as if to send Paige her love.

Tillie dabbed at her eyes with a lace-edged handkerchief.

Helen beamed, her pink dress as bright as a lighthouse beacon.

Becca and Billy stood together, their expressions solemn and a little scared.

And then there was True.

Paige didn't want to look at him until she was right in front of the altar. In her room down the hall, before the wedding march started, she had been struck with terror. She had been so afraid she would walk into this room, turn to True and see regret in his eyes.

The past week had been so busy, there hadn't been much time for them to talk. Besides the wedding preparations, she'd had to fire the ranch foreman and make decisions about whether to have him charged with embezzlement. True had a rash of fence breaks over on his place. The normal, everyday business of running two ranches took up most hours of the day. And there had been parties. A hastily arranged engagement fete last Sunday night. A shower on Friday.

Through it all, True had been right at Paige's side. But there had been no time alone. None of the persuasive kisses he had used to convince her to marry him. Little of the teasing they had always shared.

A few minutes ago, as she listened to the wedding march begin, she realized exactly what she was doing. She was marrying a man who didn't love her.

Now, as the minister spoke and her father placed her hand in True's, she finally dared look at her groom.

And in those bluebonnet blue eyes, she saw no clear reassurance for the doubts and fears winging through her. But there was no regret, either.

His hand was firm on hers.

His voice was strong when he said his vows. Stronger than hers when she responded.

His touch was warm and steady as he slipped a ring on her finger. Steadier than hers as she reciprocated.

His kiss was tender.

She had to believe in this, trust that the respect and affection he had for her would be enough.

As the kiss ended and they turned to the room full of happy, excited guests, Paige told herself to smile.

She couldn't let the panic she was feeling show on the outside. She couldn't let on that they had made a mistake.

Chapter Six

Just yesterday a quiet bed-and-breakfast had sounded like the perfect honeymoon spot to Paige. A place to be alone with True. Two days of private tranquility in which to begin their married life.

But on the drive northeast from Amarillo, Paige began to pray the inn would mix up their reservations. Maybe then she and True would have to go home, and by the time they got there, they would be exhausted. Far too exhausted to think about anything but sleep. Tomorrow, in the cold light of day, they could discuss an annulment.

Did people still get annulments, she wondered. Or was that an antiquated notion in a time when most people consummated their relationships after getting married?

"You okay?" True asked.

Paige jerked her gaze from the darkening winter landscape outside the car. "I'm fine," she assured him quickly. "Why?"

"You haven't said ten words since we left."

"I'm tired, I guess."

"We should have been on the road an hour ago, but every time we tried to leave, someone stopped us."

She didn't remember much about the hours after the ceremony. She had been hugged a lot. She thought she had eaten cake and something more, though it might have been hay for all the flavor she recalled. All too soon, Kathryn had been helping her change.

The usual customs had been observed. Paige had tossed her bouquet, caught by a startled Devon. She and True had run from the house through a hail of birdseed. They left with the bumper of her compact car trailing tin cans and other assorted noisemakers, which True had dispensed with once they were out of sight of the Double M.

True broke the silence once more. "It was a nice wedding."

She hadn't expected to hear him say that, given his reluctance to have a "fuss" made.

"I hope you were happy with it," he added.

"Of course I was."

"I want everything about today and tonight to be just right, just as special as you hoped."

Something in the emphasis he placed on "everything" sent a shiver through Paige. He might not be referring to sex, but that was what she was thinking of. Not an unusual subject for a bride anticipating her wedding night. But it was the last subject Paige wanted to consider.

That wasn't strictly correct. With all her heart, she wanted to go into True's arms tonight, give herself to him in just the way she had always dreamed. The dreaming was the problem. All of those fantasies had featured the one component missing from the reality—True's love.

She glanced at him, swallowed and tried to find her voice. She was going to tell him to turn around and take her home.

"There's the inn," he said before she could speak. "Looks as interesting as Kathryn said."

Silently cursing her best friend's helpfulness, Paige didn't reply while True guided the car up the driveway of a Victorian farmhouse. Welcoming light streamed from windows. Tall, sturdy and white against the evening sky, the house possessed the requisite gingerbread trim, cupolas, eyebrow windows, numerous porches and architectural flourishes of its era.

According to Kathryn, the house had been in a sad state of disrepair when the owners purchased it a few years ago. They did the restoration themselves, and now the inn was their home as well as a favorite lodging for tourists who came to enjoy the recreation opportunities of nearby Lake Meredith. Along with the inn, they were also involved in breeding horses, and maintained a riding stable. Late spring, summer and fall were their busy seasons, but guests were welcome year-round.

True pulled the car to a stop in a space near the

front porch. "Looks like we might be the only ones here tonight."

So much for reservation mix-ups, Paige thought. Her stomach fluttered with nerves as True got out of the car.

They were met at the door by the middle-aged husband and wife innkeepers. Pleasant and friendly, the couple escorted them to a beautiful room on the second floor.

"Our honeymoon suite," the wife, Clara, explained with a twinkle in her eye. She proudly showed off the tall four-poster bed, the chintz-covered love seat by the small fireplace and the huge claw-foot tub in a luxurious bathroom that also boasted a lighted dressing table and a shower.

On the table near the love seat, a bottle of champagne was on ice, and a dozen yellow roses were arranged in a crystal vase.

The husband, Wayne, gestured toward the flowers and said to True, "Just as you requested, I hope."

Paige looked at True in astonishment as he voiced his approval. Champagne and roses weren't his style. Or were they? Aside from several hundred shared childhood memories, what did she know about this man whose heavy band of gold and diamonds she now wore? This man who was her husband.

Before she could get too caught up in her thoughts, Clara said, "I've prepared a light supper for you. When would you like it?"

"About half an hour?" True glanced at Paige, who agreed with a nod because she couldn't force any words around the constriction in her throat.

"Let us know if there's anything you need before then." With a warm smile, their host took his wife's arm and they left True and Paige alone.

In the honeymoon suite.

Their honeymoon suite.

Paige's joints unfroze as she did a slow turn in the center of the room, taking in the soft pink and yellow of the floral wallpaper and fabrics, the muted light from the mauve fringed lamp beside the bed. The scene was set for romance.

What would True do if she jumped out of the window?

His touch on her arm startled her so that she gave a small cry.

"Hey, there," he murmured low against her ear. "I didn't mean to scare you."

Taking a deep breath, she started to face him, but the velvet glide of something soft across her cheek stopped her. A rose, she realized, turning the rest of the way to look up at him in surprise.

"I thought yellow roses were appropriate for a Texas bride."

Touched, she took the blossom he proffered. "They're beautiful."

"No prettier than you," he whispered, then kissed her.

But even with his lips on hers she couldn't relax. She eased out of his arms and gestured toward the bathroom. "I'd like to freshen up before we eat. Mind if I get in there for a bit?"

If he realized just how jumpy and reluctant she

was, he didn't show it. "Go right ahead. I think I'm going to light this fire. It's a cold night out."

Escaping with her small suitcase and toiletry bag to the bathroom, Paige closed the door and leaned against it, breathing hard. She could see her reflection in the gilt-framed mirror across the room. How foolish she looked. A thirty-one-year-old virgin with big eyes and messy hair clutching a yellow rose.

What was True going to say when she told him she was a virgin?

She had lied to him. The night he proposed she led him to believe there had been all kinds of men in her life. He was probably expecting a hot night with an experienced woman. He would get nothing of the sort. She would be letting him down right from the start. He had said he wanted a full marriage, a mutually satisfying union. That had been part of the deal. And when she accepted his proposal, she had believed that was possible. His kisses had roused a passion inside her that she had never experienced with anyone else, the sort of passion she had imagined she would feel when she finally gave herself to someone. Yet, without love…

She had wanted to be with True since she was a fifteen-year-old tomboy finally acknowledging the deep and complex differences between males and females. Suddenly she had understood why all the other girls sighed over True. Telling him how she felt hadn't seemed necessary. Though he cut a swath through the girls in high school, he always had time for Paige, as well. The twinges of jealousy she felt were easily overcome. She told herself he secretly preferred her company, and some day he would see her in a new light. Then he went off to college and met Marcie. End of Paige's dreams.

Until now.

But it was still a dream only half-fulfilled.

All these years she had saved herself for a special person, a special night. Her tales of other men hadn't been complete lies. She had dated. And dated. She had played the field, just not in the bedroom. The diamond tennis bracelet she had flaunted to True was a gift from a wealthy resort guest from South America. Javier had pursued her with a steady campaign of romantic gestures and sexy promises. He had come closer than anyone else to tempting Paige into relinquishing her innocence. When it came down to it, however, she knew it wasn't right. She didn't love him. He didn't love her.

Most of all, he wasn't True.

Respectful of her decision, Javier had told Paige she deserved someone who would offer her his heart. True had given her his name, would give her his body. But his heart...

Sternly she took hold of her runaway wishes. She told her reflection, "You idiot. You married him. You promised him this would be a real marriage, and that's what you want. He never promised you love."

Paige looked down at the ring on her left hand. She had left it up to True to pick this out all on his own, but the heavy twist of gold with a slash of diamonds suited her just fine. He suited her.

Holding on to that thought, she set about preparing

herself for the night she had been dreaming of for more than sixteen years.

True stared at the closed bathroom door. Paige had been in there a long time. He had heard the shower cut off at least fifteen minutes ago. Not long after that the innkeeper brought up the tray of food and left it on the table beside the champagne. True had been pacing the room since then, pulling off his tie, then putting it back on. He turned out most of the lights, turned them on, then cut half of them again. He tried not to look at the bed, with the comforter turned back on fancy lace-edged sheets, the pillows plumped and welcoming.

He wished he didn't feel so awkward. Paige had been quiet and jumpy on the drive up, and he hadn't known what to say. He wanted to say the right things, do the right things. Before God, family and friends, he had vowed to care for Paige. To True's way of thinking and the way he lived his life, that vow was an unbreakable bond.

Most of all, he had to respect Paige's feelings for him. Marriage called for some tenderness, some romance, some wooing. He could do that. Hell, he could enjoy that. He cared about Paige. He wanted her, too. He didn't mind contemplating the hours to come in that big, soft bed.

But why was she locked in that damn bathroom?

Crossing the room, he tapped on the door. "You okay in there?"

"Just a minute" came her faint reply.

"Dinner's here, and the ice is melting around the champagne."

"Half a second, I promise."

Mouth thinning, he jerked off his tie for a second time, tossed it across the back of a chair while he undid the top buttons of his white shirt. He wasn't about to let perfectly good champagne get warm, especially when he could use a drink. Turning his back on the bathroom door, he picked up the champagne bottle and popped the cork. He was reaching for a crystal flute when he heard a door open behind him.

He turned around and almost dropped the champagne. For a minute, he couldn't say a word. Paige's white gown shimmered in the muted glow from the lamps and the fire. He didn't know if it was silk or satin or something else, but whatever the material was it clung to every dip and curve of her slender body. Enhancing the thoroughly feminine illusion was a sheer, sleeveless robe.

"Wow" was all he could come up with.

She laughed, a nervous sound.

Rapidly recovering his poise and his enthusiasm for the night they were about to share, he said simply, "You're worth waiting for."

"I'm sorry about that." Paige fiddled with the rose she carried. "I didn't mean to take so long."

"No problem," he lied as he filled both flutes with champagne. "Come and eat. I'm sure you're as hungry as I am. There was too much going on at the reception to do more than grab a bite."

She hesitated a moment more before coming forward and taking her champagne.

"Sit here, close to the fire. The room's drafty." He indicated one end of the love seat, then sat down and pulled covers off the tray of food on the table. There was fruit and roasted chicken, cheese and bread. Chocolate truffles for dessert. "Looks good, doesn't it?"

She slipped her rose back in the vase with the others. "Very."

He held up his flute. "First a toast." He touched the glass to hers, caught and held her deep brown-eyed gaze. "To beginnings."

She managed a grin before echoing the toast and sipping her champagne. True realized it was the first time he had seen her smile since they had arrived at the inn. He took her hand. "Is this place all right with you? I know you're used to a four-star resort, but this sounded nice when Kathryn described it. I'm no judge, obviously, but it seems—"

"It's beautiful," she interrupted hastily. "And there's not a thing wrong. Let's eat and enjoy our champagne."

After that, she kept up a running stream of conversation. Small talk, mostly. About the wedding. The twins. Her father and the problems at the McMullen spread. She talked a lot and didn't eat much. True just listened, mostly, gradually letting himself relax.

Well, relax wasn't the right word. He found it next to impossible to be completely laid-back when she was sitting so close to him, looking the way she looked in that gown.

While she was going on about her plans to upgrade the Double M stock, he was studying the satin strap that kept slipping down one of her arms. If it fell just a little bit farther, the top of the gown would slip, perhaps exposing the nipple pearling so prettily beneath the sleek material that covered her breasts. He could imagine how that small, hardening nub would feel to his fingertips. To his tongue—

"True?"

With a guilty start, he jerked his gaze back to her face. "Yeah?" His voice was dismayingly husky.

"I asked if you knew anyone who might want the foreman's job."

He blinked. "The foreman?"

"At the ranch."

"But I already have—"

"Not at your place. At the Double M."

He shook his head to clear it. "I'm sure your dad knows someone."

"I'm doing the hiring."

"Well...I don't know." After setting his plate and glass aside, True disposed of hers, as well. Then he got her hand again and lifted it to his lips. "Do you really want to talk about the ranch right now?"

She took a deep breath, and that strap slipped another inch down her arm. True turned her hand over and pressed his mouth to her palm. Paige's eyes closed as he opened his lips and trailed his tongue up to her wrist. She smelled of some sweet and spicy perfume, faintly exotic, altogether arousing.

He moved closer. "I like your perfume. It's different than what you used to wear."

Her eyes opened, though the lids appeared heavy

and the pupils unfocused. "You remember what I used to wear?"

"It came in a peach box. Aunt Helen made me give it to you once for Christmas."

He put his hand on her arm, just over the sliding strap, his body stirring at the warmth of her skin. He slipped his arm around her shoulder and lowered his mouth toward hers. "You wore it on Sunday mornings when you and Tillie picked me up for church. I thought it was nice."

"Just nice?" she murmured, her mouth almost under his.

"Not as nice as this," he replied before his lips touched hers.

The kiss went from tender to deep almost immediately. The scant distance between them disappeared, as well. But as fast as her body went pliant next to his, she stiffened again. She was up and out of his arms with a move that threatened to turn over the table of roses, champagne and food.

True got to his feet and came around the table, concerned by her agitation. "What's wrong?"

She turned away, covering her face with her hands.

He touched her shoulder. "Paige?"

Dropping her hands from her face, she faced him. Her eyes were big and filled with tears. "I don't think I can do this."

He drew back, not sure what she meant.

"I can't make love with you."

A kick to the kidneys wouldn't have caught him as off guard as this. "What?"

"I just can't. I know you're going to be angry. I know I should have told you before."

"Before?" he repeated, hands going to his hips as he stared at her. "You mean you've been thinking about this?"

"Not until today."

"Today? But we got married today."

"That's when I started thinking about what we were doing, about what marriage would really mean."

"Wait a minute." He held up his hand, trying to make sense of what she was saying. "You sound as if you hadn't thought about it before now."

She walked away, drawing her sheer robe tight around her middle. "It didn't hit me until today how awkward all this could be. Especially this."

"This?"

"Being with you tonight."

Irritation heated his face. "I thought this was what you wanted? A real marriage. Children."

"I do want that." Her expression was pure misery. "I think."

"You think?" His voice rose against his will.

Paige shushed him. "Don't yell at me."

He took a deep breath. "If you call *this* yelling, just wait…"

For several moments, they stared at each other. His belly was burning. She was breathing hard, her breasts moving beneath that damned sexy gown. A gown she had apparently worn just to torture him.

Holding tight to the reins of his anger, he said, "I don't get this."

"I'm sorry. I didn't intend to react this way. I

thought I could go through with it. Just grit my teeth—"

"Grit your teeth?" he demanded, voice rising again despite her protests. "You sound as if you were expecting me to torture you."

"That's not it—"

"If I remember correctly, you weren't gritting your teeth that morning we decided to get married. Or the night outside my house. Or even a few minutes ago."

"But you've barely touched me all week."

"You were embroiled in *your* wedding plans."

"*My* wedding?" she retorted, eyes snapping.

He backed off, shoving hands in the pockets of his dark dress jeans in an effort to keep calm. "Okay, so we were both busy."

"We haven't been alone all week. That makes me feel weird about tonight."

Frustration sparked inside him again. "Then why are you prissing around here in that gown?"

"Prissing?" she repeated. "I've never prissed in my entire life."

"Maybe I should have called it teasing."

"I'm not a tease, either."

"You're dressed like one."

"That's not fair. Just because I'm not sure about this—"

"Not sure? If you're not sure, then what the hell are we doing here?"

With a succinct, emphatic curse, she whirled away from him again. "It's nice to learn that you married me just for the sex."

"Too bad if I did, right?"

"Don't be a smart-ass."

"Then don't be one with me. You know I didn't marry you just to sleep with you. But I also don't plan on sleeping in twin beds like Lucy and Ricky Ricardo."

She moved around the room, not looking at him. "Can't we wait?"

"For what?"

"Until I'm ready."

"Ready?"

"For when we're used to each other."

He opened his mouth, but no sound escaped. She had knocked him totally off-balance. She had taken the same vows as he had this afternoon, but now she claimed to be full of doubts. One minute she had been in his arms, responding to him. The next she was saying she wasn't ready to be with him, that she needed time to become used to someone she had known forever. His disappointment wasn't about sex; it was about their marriage not getting off to the sort of start he had wanted.

To think he had worried about making tonight so special. He thought she was in love with him, that he needed to be sensitive to her feelings. He had agonized over a choice of flowers, made a special effort to order them and the champagne. He had called Kathryn twice, just to reassure himself that the inn was the perfect place for him and Paige to start their marriage.

But maybe that was it. Maybe it wasn't perfect. Or even good enough.

The acid burning in his gut turned his words bitter.

"I guess some other man would have flown you to Hawaii or something?"

She spun back to look at him. "What?"

"The kind of man who gave you that diamond bracelet would have flown you to some tropical place for your honeymoon. That guy wouldn't have tried to impress you with flowers and champagne and a honeymoon suite. He'd have rented a villa...or a chalet...or whatever the hell you call houses rich people rent."

Paige was shaking her head.

But True was too worked up to listen to any denials. "I'm sorry I can't do that, Paige. This is the best I could do. I've got a ranch to run and kids to look after and other uses for what little money I have. I guess that's what really hit you today, isn't it? All that I don't have."

"That's ridiculous. I've never even thought about what you have."

He didn't believe her. "I shouldn't be surprised. You were raised rich, while we were just trying to get by over at our place."

"That never mattered to me. It doesn't now."

He took a step toward her, hands fisted at his sides. "Then maybe it's not my lack of money at all. Maybe it's my technique. You can tell me what all your rich, perfect lovers did to get you *used* to them."

She backed up. "Stop it, True."

Ignoring her, he challenged, "Tell me. Spell it out. What is it you like? Something kinky? I may be just a good old Texas boy, but I'm willing—"

"There weren't any other lovers."

"Oh, yeah, right. Is that the game you're playing? Some kind of virgin-meets-cowboy routine?" He pulled her back into his arms. "If that's the role you want—"

"It's no role." Muscles worked in her throat. "I am a virgin, True."

"And I'm a movie star. Tom Cruise or Brad Pitt. Take your pick."

"Stop it." Paige pushed hard against his chest. "Listen to me. I've never slept with anyone."

He started to laugh and protest again. But there was something in her expression that made him stop. He had always known when Paige was lying. She wasn't now. In her eyes, in her trembling lips, he read the facts. She was telling him the God's honest truth.

"Holy—" He leapt back. If she had burned him, he couldn't have moved any faster.

"That's why I wasn't going to tell you," she said, arms falling awkwardly to her sides. "Because I knew you would look at me like that."

"But you said...you seemed..." Confused, True put a hand to his forehead and stared at her. "Christ, Paige, you're thirty-one."

"So what?"

"So there must have been men."

"There were," she assured him, chin lifting to a defiant tilt. "Plenty of men."

"And nobody ever..."

"Got me to play the virgin and the cowboy?" She compressed her lips. "No."

Shame sent the blood rushing to True's cheeks.

"Lord, Slim, I'm sorry I said that or suggested that you…'' Miserable, he let his words fade.

She looked down at her hands. "I'm sorry I tricked you. I should have told you. I know you wish I had. You had certain…expectations.''

This was ridiculous, True realized. She was standing here, apologizing because she was a virgin. She was sorry because she had waited before sharing herself in the most intimate way possible between a man and woman. "You've got nothing to be sorry for,'' he told her, a bit more harshly than he intended. He took a breath to settle himself. "You waited for marriage. That's…special.''

When she glanced back up at him, her expression reminded him sharply of the Paige of old, the one who tried so hard to please everyone in her life. He had seen her, time and again, looking for approval. When it came, from him or Rex or Tillie, Paige used to have a smile that would break across her face…man, what a smile. As bright as Christmas tree lights on the first night they went up. He wanted that smile now.

Moving close, he took one of her hands. "Don't apologize again.''

She rewarded him with only a slight grin, a pale shadow of the smile he was searching for. Her expression was still uncertain. "I don't know why I let you think I was a woman of the world.''

"Maybe because I assumed you must be. All those years away from here. Coming home looking so sophisticated.''

"I know I'm not normal. Guys were always telling me I was weird."

"All I've got to say is that those California guys are the weird ones. They let a prize slip away."

The smile came then. As dazzling as True remembered. "Thank you for saying that," she whispered.

He kissed her forehead in reply, drawing her into his arms once more. She came willingly and tucked her head just under his chin.

God, he liked the feel of her. Her slim curves. Her soft hair. Her silky skin. Knowing she was a virgin put more pressure on him than ever. But it was a burden he could live with. In fact, it sort of…turned him on. His body stirred as he thought about being the first man to explore all her feminine secrets. The first to slip inside her, take her. The images clicked through his mind, one after the other. Each more erotic than the last.

In his arms, Paige shivered slightly, and he drew her closer. "You cold?"

"A little."

"Want to get to bed?"

She stepped back, chewing at her bottom lip as she looked up at him.

Smiling, he cupped her chin. "Don't look so scared."

"But I don't—"

His fingers against her lips silenced her. "Now that I know the truth, which you should have told me in the first place, things can be different."

"And we'll wait?"

He blinked, cleared his throat. "You want to wait?"

"We're virtual strangers, True."

"You don't..." He had to swallow. "You don't feel like a stranger to me, Slim."

"But—"

He kissed her again, tenderly, coaxingly. "This is our wedding night," he murmured.

"And I'm not ready." She stepped away from him. "You wouldn't want to force me to do anything—"

"Force?" The word snapped True out of his partially aroused haze. There was no woman in this world who could even hint at him being anything less than a gentleman. Certainly this woman, who had been raised with him, knew better. But of course, she was claiming she didn't really know him. That they were strangers. The very idea. Anger, bullwhip sharp, licked through him. "Do you honestly believe I would force you?"

"Not as in physically force, of course—"

"You're damn straight," he retorted. Leaving her standing in the middle of the room, he strode back to the table where the champagne rested in melted ice. He poured himself another glass and took a long, deep drink.

"True?" Paige's voice sounded small and uncertain.

"It's late and it's cold," he said without turning. "You ought to get to bed."

"You should, too."

He darted a glance toward the bed. "And where, pray tell, would you advise me to do that?" He turned to face her. "If you know what's good for you, you won't suggest I call up our good hosts and ask for another bed."

"You can sleep with me."

He lifted one eyebrow and poured another glass of champagne.

Paige came over and took it out of his hand. "That's enough of that."

"Are you going to leave me with no comforts on my wedding night?"

"Don't be medieval about this. We're not animals. Surely we can sleep together in that bed without you attacking me?"

He grunted, then raked an appraising look up and down her body.

She crossed her arms. "Come on, True. Don't look as if I'm putting you on the rack. All I'm asking for is a little time, some patience. I just want us to get used to each other."

"By sleeping together?" He snorted. "You really are a virgin, aren't you?"

Temper blazed from her eyes. "All right, be stubborn. See if you can sleep on this little love seat."

"I will," he retorted.

"Fine." She stomped across the floor, dropped her robe in a heap and flung back the covers. With two quick motions, she clicked off the bedside lamp and got in bed.

Cursing, True went into motion. He grabbed up his bag and retreated from the moderate warmth by the fire to the chilly bathroom. Ten minutes later, teeth brushed, clad only in boxers, he stepped back into the bedroom. Damn, but it was cold. If he had known he'd be sleeping alone, he might have brought some more suitable attire.

Shivering, he spared a nasty glance toward the blanket-covered lump in the bed. Paige had her back to him, apparently already lost in slumber. Then he poked at the fire, trying to stir some more heat from the remaining coals. That helped a little. So did wrapping himself in an afghan he found on the antique quilt rack. He shut out the rest of the lights and settled down on the love seat, propping his head on one arm. Not too bad there. Unfortunately, his feet stuck out a good half foot beyond the other arm. Beyond the afghan, too.

He twisted.

He turned.

For at least an hour, True tried to find a position he could live with on that little love seat. Damn Paige, anyway. She really had put him on the rack.

Finally, from the bed, came a weary "Would you please stop making so much noise and get in here?"

Pride be damned, True thought as he threw off the afghan and headed for the four-poster. He sighed in relief as the mattress gave beneath his weight and the blankets folded around him with comforting warmth.

"Just stick to your side," Paige instructed him, still not moving.

"Gladly." He turned his back to her. It would take an earthquake to get him near her, he told himself. A big one.

The quake didn't rouse him. But it must have happened. For when True woke to the thin light of dawn, he was pressed up against Paige. His arm was around her waist. Her bottom was snuggled into his hips. As for the big one...well, he imagined it was his own aroused state that had brought him out of a deep, dreamless sleep.

Paige, his virgin bride, slept on.

True eased away from her with great care and tried in vain to sleep. The day stretched ahead with disconcerting bleakness. When sex was off-limits, what the hell did a person do on a honeymoon in the middle of winter in a largely deserted summer resort area?

He didn't have a clue.

Paige closed the door to the honeymoon suite and stalked to the bed and back. The room, with its cheery fire and soft lights, was as welcoming tonight as last evening. But here she was, alone, while True was in the inn's parlor, playing chess with their host.

The innkeepers, Wayne and Clara, must think them the oddest honeymoon couple ever. Paige and True had taken all their meals with their hosts. True had even coaxed Wayne into joining them on a morning horseback ride. The two men had spent all their time comparing notes of horse breeding. Paige and True's only time alone came when she convinced him to go for a short drive this afternoon. They had found a couple of small antique shops to wander through and the day had begun to look up.

True had been courteous, but distant. He helped her pick out some gifts for the twins. As they looked at furniture and knickknacks, they discussed ideas for renovating his ranch house into a more comfortable home.

But he was so very careful not to touch Paige. When she casually took his arm or accidentally brushed up against him, he jerked away. Like a spring, she thought. A tightly wound spring.

Finally, when they got back to the inn, she had asked him if he just wanted to check out, go home, forget this farce of a honeymoon.

Tersely, he had told her the second night was paid for already, as if that was that.

Then he took a nap while she read a magazine.

For dinner, they had eaten a singularly delicious meal down in the dining room with Clara and Wayne. But Paige couldn't fully enjoy the food. Every time she looked up, True was watching her. His blue eyes were hooded and intense. Simmering with some unspoken emotion. He made her terribly nervous.

Nervous? She laughed. The truth was that he made her hot. Very, very hot. Halfway through dessert, she had been tempted to tell him one day of waiting was enough. She had wanted to fall into bed with him without any further getting used to each other.

But even if she gave in to that urge, all the reasons she had given True for waiting would still apply. No matter how much she wanted him, they needed to wait before progressing to the deepest level of intimacy. She had done this backward. After rushing headlong into marriage, now she needed time.

And she wanted True to court her.

She supposed this urge to be pursued and wooed was latent feminine vanity, the sort that had escaped

her most of her life. She knew she was being per-
verse—on the one hand asking True for patience, on
the other hand wanting him to chase her, attempt to
seduce her.

Seduction, however, seemed the last thing on his
mind. After dinner, True had suggested chess to
Wayne, just as if it was normal for a man on the
second night of his honeymoon to prefer a stranger's
company to his bride's.

An uncomfortable little voice down inside Paige
reminded her she had only herself to blame for her
honeymoon blues. She had a sneaking suspicion she
would have to ask, right out, before True approached
her again.

"Damn," she told the room. "Double damn."

Stubbornly, however, she reminded herself that
True was behaving like a schoolboy whose ball game
had been rained out. His game of choice canceled, he
chose to sulk rather than find a new pastime.

When she had said she wanted to wait, wanted
them to get used to each other before consummating
their marriage, she hadn't meant for him to withdraw
completely. Couldn't he at least kiss her? Touch her?

"Oh, bother," she murmured aloud. With a frustrated sigh, she wandered around the room. Through
the open door to the bathroom, she spied the big,
claw-footed tub. A good long soak would be nice, she
told herself. It beat waiting around for her missing
groom.

A few minutes later, she slipped into a rapidly filling tub. The bath crystals thoughtfully provided by
their hosts made fragrant bubbles all around her. The

warm water closed around her tired muscles, easing her tension and frustration. She leaned back, closing her eyes.

Maybe it was the running water. Maybe it was the lethargy flooding through her. For whatever reason, she didn't hear the bathroom door creak open. She didn't realize True was standing on the threshold until he spoke.

"Looks like you have room for me."

The husky observation brought Paige to splashing alertness. Then she sank down again, her arms crossing over her breasts. "What are you doing?"

Calmly, True pulled off one cowboy boot and then another.

"True?" she demanded, her voice nothing more than a squeak.

He pulled his shirttail from his jeans and unbuckled his belt. "I think I want a bath."

"Take a shower."

He cocked an eyebrow over blue eyes smoldering with the same intensity he had teased her with all during dinner. "I prefer a tub."

"Then I'll get out."

He shed the shirt, belt and his socks, and went to work on the zipper of his jeans. "Excuse me," he drawled. "Didn't you say you wanted us to get to know each other better?"

Though that was exactly what she had been wishing for only moments ago, Paige protested, "I meant we should talk."

Shoving his jeans down his long, firm-muscled legs, he laughed. "Slim, darlin', those looks you were throwing at me all during dinner didn't have nothing to do with talking.''

She gulped, tried to form a protest. Honesty stopped her. Or maybe it was True's motions that stopped her. For he dispensed with his jockey shorts as quickly as he had his jeans.

He stood there, impressively naked. Fully aroused. And coming toward her.

''Make room, baby. I'm coming in.''

Chapter Seven

True grinned as he walked toward the man-size, claw-footed tub. Try as she might, Paige couldn't keep herself completely covered with bubbles, arms or hands, making it possible for him to enjoy the peekaboo views of lightly freckled shoulders, pale breasts and long legs. His body responded predictably to the delectable, feminine sight. Paige's eyes widened at his reaction.

He didn't intend to embarrass her, but he'd be damned if this marriage was going to continue progressing like a first date. If she wanted them to get to know each other, he was game. But he was going to set the pace.

Unhurried, he bent over, turned off the water and watched the crimson in Paige's cheeks spread down her throat. "What's the matter, Slim?" he drawled. "It's not like you've never seen me naked."

She sputtered and tried to pretend she wasn't checking him out. "You were about seven."

"Oh, yeah." He glanced down at himself, then back at her with a smile. "I guess things have changed."

In response, Paige splashed him, the drop in her guard and hands providing an enticing glimpse of one pink-tipped breast.

He shook his head at her. "I don't believe Wayne or Clara would appreciate a flood up here."

"Then you'd better not get in this tub."

Ignoring her warning, he ambled to the end of the tub and stepped in behind her. Still protesting, she doubled up like an accordion, modesty or some other cautionary emotion keeping her from jumping up. True slipped down in the water, grateful for the depth and width of the tub as he stretched his legs around Paige's body.

She darted a furious look over one scrunched-up shoulder. "I don't know what you're trying to prove."

He settled back against the tub with a sigh. "I think this is nice."

"I think you're crazy."

True reached out and trailed a finger down her spine. She shivered and tried in vain to wiggle farther away.

"Come on now," he coaxed. He gently took hold of her arm. "Slide back here and relax."

She looked as if he were suggesting she jump into

pig slop. He inclined slightly and placed both hands on her slim shoulders. Though she resisted for a moment, tension soon left her body, and she allowed True to pull her with him as he relaxed once more against the back of the tub.

The combination of her sleek, soft skin and the warm, fragrant water stirred True's senses to full life. Paige's bottom moved against his groin, and she glanced around at him again, brown eyes rounding.

Smiling, he slipped his arms around her, his hands resting just beneath the swell of her breasts. Tendrils of strawberry blond hair had darkened to light cinnamon from the water and steam. They trailed from the lopsided bun she had drawn to the crown of her head. He bent forward, resting his forehead against her neck as he breathed in her scent. "You smell nice. Like roses."

"It's the bath crystals," Paige offered, still sounding stiff, even though her body was gradually softening.

True pressed a kiss to her right shoulder. "Good to see you still have freckles."

"Where would they have gone?"

"I don't know. A lot of other things have changed about the way you look."

She shook her head. "You didn't think so that first day we ran into each other at the supply store."

"Not at first," True admitted. But all too clearly, he remembered how his fingers had accidentally brushed across her breasts that day. The very breasts that pillowed so enticingly near now. He had only to turn his palms up and…just like that, he was cupping her breasts.

Paige released a long, audible breath. But she didn't protest. She didn't jerk away. If anything, it felt as if the last bit of fight went out of her. She sank lower in the water and back against him.

He rotated his hands, savoring the distinct pebbling of her nipples in his palms. Again, he kissed her shoulder. "Is this such a bad way to get to know each other?"

"It's not exactly what I meant."

"So why aren't you leaving?"

"Would you let me?"

"No one's forcing you to stay."

But she didn't move away or try to leave. As he continued to encircle the tips of her breasts with his thumbs, Paige turned her head slightly toward him. Her only answer to his question was another sigh of pleasure.

He grinned. "I think this qualifies as a great get-acquainted activity. Part of the courting ritual is petting, you know."

"In the bathtub?"

"You want to get dressed and go get in the back seat of the car?"

Paige chuckled. "No."

He allowed one hand to slide from her breast to her waist, down to the flare of one hip. "You want me to stop what I'm doing?"

She twisted partway around and looked up at him. "You want to stop?"

In reply, he captured her lips beneath his. He kissed

her tenderly at first, just nibbling at her mouth. Then she opened to him, one of her hands reaching up to touch his face while the kiss deepened.

True took most of her weight along one leg and turned so that she was almost facing him. He felt the frustration of the confines of the tub. The kiss got wilder, and he let his hands roam at will. Over her breasts again. Up and down one silky thigh. Tracing the smooth curve of her bottom. The firm flesh of her stomach. Lower. Moving toward the cleft between her legs.

At that touch, she broke the kiss, one hand halting his progress low on her body. Her eyes were closed. Her breathing had quickened. He could feel her heart pounding as hard as his own. Despite the effects of the warm, languid water, he was fully erect, a fact she couldn't help but notice given the intimacy of their postures.

When Paige opened her eyes, he could read a question in those brown, velvet depths. Instead of saying anything, however, she rested her head against his shoulder. Her fingers threaded through the damp patch of dark hair on his chest. True's body tightened even more as her fingertips grazed one nipple, then the other. He came damn close to exploding when she leaned over and let her lips take over that slight, tantalizing action. Then her hand dipped beneath the water and hesitated low on his belly.

"You're headed in the right direction," he murmured, his voice strained.

She looked up at him again, expression teasing. "Am I?"

Anticipation froze his vocal chords so that he could only nod.

Instead of proceeding with her explorations, Paige just continued smiling and drawing circles with her fingertips on his stomach.

A few moments of that were all True could stand. He took over, gently guiding her hand to his thickened shaft.

She drew in a breath that escaped very slowly. Her gaze was focused downward. Her fingers tightened and relaxed around him. Once. Twice. Too many times to count.

True had to hang on to the sides of the tub to keep from disappearing beneath the water. But he managed a weak smile. "Find something you like, Slim?"

"I think..." She peeked up at him once more. "I think...this water is getting awfully cold." With that, she let go of him, grasped the edges of the tub and got to her feet.

If she thought to cool his ardor, her move was all wrong. Because watching Paige come up out of that water, with her skin all pink and gold and wet, was as arousing as any touch.

As she turned, her arms crossed protectively over her breasts, but that left him with a clear view of long, slim legs, gently rounded hips and the gingery triangle at the juncture of her thighs. Then she was out of the tub, reaching for a towel, grinning at him just as she had when she was a teasing, taunting kid, eager to elude him in a game of chase.

True came after her, water cascading off his body like a waterfall.

"Now you're causing a flood." As she backed away, Paige tucked the towel around her torso, securing it between her breasts.

He lifted his arms. "Care to dry me?"

Her response was to throw him a towel. He avoided it, and moved toward her. She wheeled away, laughing when he caught her just outside the bathroom door. That laughter turned to squeals when he picked her up and hefted her over his shoulder. Four strides brought them to the bed, where he dumped her onto the soft, thick comforter. Her towel peeled away as prettily as the petals of a flower. He tossed it aside.

Paige scrambled to cover herself, but True was beside her quickly, pushing her hands away, replacing them with his own and kissing her protests into silence.

He was still wet. The room was chilly. But holding Paige's damp, warm body brought him the sweetest of heat. He kissed her lips, her breasts, the pale skin of her stomach. With his gaze fastened on hers he brushed his fingers through the curls that guarded her feminine mound.

She gasped when one finger breached her cleft. Her knees came up; her protest was automatic. "True, we agreed—"

"To take it slow," he murmured, kissing her again. "I promise to do exactly that." At the same time, his probing fingers found and circled the sensitive kernel of flesh deep in the folds of her body. She jerked, but didn't draw away. He moved his lips to her breasts, intensified the pressure of his fingers. Her legs eased apart. Her hips arched upward. He brought her to one

peak. Then another. Until she was gasping, holding
on to his shoulders, calling his name.

He could have taken her then. One stroke, one
movement of his body, and she would have been his
wife in fact, as well as name. He let himself imagine
pumping into her, spilling into the body that was so
completely, so prettily, open to him.

But he didn't.

He kissed her, instead. He watched her slide down
from the pinnacle of her climax. He held her. He felt
her breath return to normal, her skin cool. Finally, he
settled them both under the sheets and comforter. He
decided there was something pretty damn sexy about
this waiting she had imposed. There were all kinds of
ways to make each other feel good. Each of them was
the sort of thing a man and woman did when they
were courting, when they were anticipating the plea-
sures of marriage.

"Just think," he whispered low against her ear.
"Think how great it's going to be when I'm inside
you."

Paige's shiver had nothing to do with the temperature in the room. She turned to face him. "It's hard
to imagine anything better than what I just felt."

"Multiply it by ten."

"I'll die."

"I'll chance it."

His grin was so perfect, so *True*. She was com-
pelled to kiss him. Kisses led to touches. Soon he was
lying on his back, his distinctly masculine, unbeliev-
ably taut body spread for her investigation.

She indulged herself. She guided her hands over

the long muscles of his arms and legs. She savored the lingering scent of bath crystals on his skin. She allowed her lips to follow the hair that whorled from the center of his chest to a thin line down his flat belly.

And when her hands finally closed over his heavy, jutting sex, she brought him to release in much the same way he had pleasured her.

As the last tremors spread through him, he pulled her on top of him, their bodies fitting intimately together. He protested when she tried to draw away.

Braced by her arms, she remained just above him. "Now, True Whitman, you know what they told us in health class. Penetration does not have to occur for a pregnancy to result."

He pulled her hair free of its bun, so that it swung down on either side of her face and grazed his cheeks. "I see it this way," he whispered, tucking the still-damp strands behind her ears. "If some sperm of mine has enough spunk to survive out in the open and swim all that way…well, more power to the little sucker."

Laughing, she allowed herself to relax against him. It just seemed right, them lying together this way. Paige was warm and content, her arms crossed on True's chest, her head pillowed near his. She felt like talking. "You know, as long as we're on this subject…"

"What subject?" His eyes were closed and he sounded sleepy.

"Sperm and eggs. Birth control."

He opened one eye. "Were we discussing that?"

"It's just one of the many subjects we should have gone over before we got married."

His brow crinkled. "I guess I assumed I would be taking care of it for now." Ruefully, he added, "But then, I assumed this honeymoon would go a little different, as well."

"We should have talked about this," Paige said. "I'm not just blaming you. I should have insisted we slow down and talk a lot of things over." To herself, she admitted she had been too afraid he would back out of the wedding to try to apply the brakes too strenuously.

With a heavy sigh, he turned their bodies so she was lying beside him. He was on his side, his arm bracing his head. Again he brushed her hair away from her face. "You're right."

Paige was surprised to hear that admission from him.

He chuckled and kissed her. "Don't look so stunned. I am capable of admitting when someone has the right idea."

"I'll have to let Aunt Helen know you said that."

"And we probably should have waited to get married," he admitted, blue eyes serious.

Paige couldn't stop the sudden panic that seized her gut. "So are you sorry?"

He shook his head. "I still think it was the right move for both of us. I believe we can be happy."

"I want to be," she murmured, touching his cheek. "I know I sprang a couple of surprises on you last night."

"You were right to suggest we get...adjusted to

each other." He grinned at her again. "I sort of like this adjusting."

"Last night I was panicked, thinking about all of...well..." Her gaze fell from his, hot color flooding her cheeks as she thought about the past half hour. "About all of this. I got nervous and worried that I wouldn't please you, that we had made a mistake."

"We can work through this. I was sure of that when I came and joined you in the tub."

She snuggled closer to his side. "I guess that was a good move."

"This won't go any further until you're ready," he murmured. "We can take all the time you need."

She had been right, Paige thought. Since she had asked for this waiting period, True would leave the decision of when to make love completely up to her. The thought of going beyond what had happened between them tonight made her head spin. The thought of asking for more was unimaginable. But surely it would just happen. Naturally. Just as it could have tonight. She was well aware he could have taken advantage of her arousal tonight. His holding back touched her, made her all the more eager to know the full measure of sexual pleasure with him.

To remain strong, she had to keep reminding herself of why she had asked him to wait. They needed to establish some emotional intimacy. She wanted exactly the sort of closeness that would grow from this kind of pillow talk. True might never love her, but there had been too much haste between them already. They needed this time.

"Thank you," she told True. "For understanding. For being patient with me."

His expression was roguish as he slid his hand down her side, fingers just brushing the curve of her breast. "There are limits to my patience."

She turned on her back, shifting away from him even as she edged the conversation in another direction. "There are a couple of dozen other things we need to consider about this marriage." She bit her lip, then continued. "I know you keep telling me not to worry about the twins, but—"

"They won't be a problem."

"But, True..." Hesitating only briefly, she told him some of what Helen had shared about Becca's need for attention and Billy's predisposition toward mischief. While Helen hadn't come right out and said it, Paige believed the older woman didn't think her capable of handling the children and their problems.

Just as Helen had said, True didn't seem to think there was a problem with them. "Aunt Helen worries too much. You're going to be great for the kids."

"But we haven't sorted anything out about schedules or anything. And I don't know the kids well enough to know how I should discipline them. *If* I should discipline—"

"It'll come to you," he interrupted. "I trust you to always do right by them. Just trust your judgment. I will."

"But we're going to be so busy. I'll be over at the ranch a lot."

"I'll be working, too. The kids will be in school.

We'll all get adjusted to one another's schedules. It will be fine.''

"But—"

"We'll work it out," True said with his usual confidence. Tenderly, he massaged her shoulder, kissed her with the utmost tenderness. "Don't worry. We'll take everything just like we're taking this. One step at a time."

It sounded so simple when he reassured her. So sane. So right. Paige fell asleep in his arms, feeling strong and capable, confident about their future. The feeling lasted all the way until the next morning, until after they shared a leisurely breakfast with their hosts and drove away from the cocooned environment of the inn.

Paige couldn't help but dart a wistful glance over her shoulder as the big, old Victorian house faded from sight. She was smart enough to know the reality she and True were driving toward wasn't nearly as tranquil as what they were leaving behind.

By after nine that night, Paige sat on the edge of the bed she was going to share with True, staring at an assortment of boxes and suitcases and wondering how she was going to find the strength to root out even the basic necessities. She supposed it helped that she hadn't quite had time to settle in at the Double M before deciding to marry True. Many of her things from her place in California had never been unpacked.

From the doorway, Aunt Helen said, "You look plumb tuckered out."

"It's been quite a day," Paige admitted.

After leaving the inn that morning, she and True had stopped first to see her father. Rex had looked stronger and healthier, changed for the better in just the two days Paige and True had been away. Paige realized that Tillie and True had been right to say her father needed independence and work to do instead of coddling.

Rex had been waiting to interview a candidate for ranch foreman. So True had taken a load of boxes to his place and left Paige to talk with the prospective employee, as well.

After the interview, she and Rex made a joint decision to hire the young man, who had worked at a ranch in the region for several years and came highly recommended. Paige felt good about the way her father had listened to her, and the way they had worked together. Rex said he was eager for them to make plans for the busy tourist season, now only a couple of months away. He wanted Paige's input, gave weight to her opinions.

Paige got so caught up in discussions and plans with Rex, she had let time slip away. It was after four and the twins were home from school before she arrived at the Circle W with an additional load of clothes and other possessions.

True had clearly been displeased that she hadn't been home to greet Becca and Billy. Paige could see his point, since it was their first day home after the wedding. But she also noted that the kids had little to say to her. They weren't hostile, but not exactly welcoming, either. Though they helped her unload her car with a minimum of fuss, they went about their after-school chores as if she wasn't there.

Helen had almost made up for their coolness, greeting Paige with an affectionate hug and kiss. She and Tillie had engineered a nice surprise in the house. All of Helen's belongings had been transported to the efficiency apartment waiting for her in Lubbock. Her empty rooms had been filled with furniture Paige had shipped from her apartment in California. For the few days Helen would remain at the ranch, she had moved to the first-floor guest bedroom at the front of the house.

While the rooms Helen had vacated still sported outdated flocked wallpaper and worn carpet, Paige was pleased to see the simple, familiar lines of her Shaker-style bed. Her plushly cushioned love seat, easy chair and other furniture fit the sitting room perfectly. This arrangement gave her and True a private retreat.

Though the change had been her idea, Helen now cast a worried frown at Paige. "I sure hope you don't mind me and Tillie going ahead and doing this."

"Of course not," Paige replied, surprised. "I'm grateful."

Still Helen seemed concerned. "What does True think about the change?"

"I'm sure he likes it," Paige said, then frowned, suddenly uncertain. The afternoon and evening had passed in a blur. True had some business to attend to while Paige and the twins unloaded her car. Helen had prepared a special welcome home meal. Then there had been presents for the kids and the older woman to open. Dishes to do. Homework. In all of that time, had True said anything about the change in his sleeping arrangements? Paige honestly didn't know.

"I just thought it would be for the best," Helen continued. "You two are newlyweds. You need a place to be alone. And then…" Her teasing grin was remarkably like True's. "Well, this sitting room might make a real nice nursery sometime soon. At least I hope it's soon. That's the other reason I wanted to put you off by yourselves. I want you to get busy on a baby before I kick the bucket."

Paige's face heated, then burned when True stepped to Helen's side in the doorway.

Grinning easily at Paige, he looped an arm around his elderly relative. "How dare you, Aunt Helen, making my bride blush like that."

Helen's laughter was hearty. "Chances are she'll get over that blushing soon enough, being married to the likes of you."

Cursing her scarlet-flushed cheeks, Paige pushed herself off the bed and got busy trying to push a large wardrobe box out of the way of the closet door. "What I wish, Helen, is that you wouldn't talk about kicking the bucket like that."

"That's right," True said, coming over to assist Paige. "You're going to have us even more worried about you moving off to Lubbock. We might have to insist you stay here so we can look after you."

"Oh, no, you don't." Helen's hands fisted on her ample hips. "I'm going off to spend my golden years in peace and quiet. I'll come help when your babies arrive. After that, you're welcome to visit every once in a while. But that's all.''

Paige and True laughed at her typical bluntness. From behind Aunt Helen, however, a voice said, "Is Paige having a baby?"

The question came from a pajama-clad Billy, who stood in the doorway, blue eyes wide, accompanied by a frowning Becca. Both True and Helen had apparently been struck dumb, a development startling in the other woman.

So Paige was left to formulate an answer. "No, I am not having a baby. We were all just joking about babies.''

Sticking her hands in the pockets of her blue-flowered robe, Becca asked, "Are you *ever* having a baby?" Her tone of elaborate unconcern didn't fool Paige for one minute.

Knowing this was a question she wouldn't touch, Paige looked at True. He cleared his throat, then hesitated.

Aunt Helen chuckled. "If you will excuse me, I'm going to bed and let you handle this." The older woman's laughter could be heard all the way through the sitting room, the back hall and kitchen.

The two blue-eyed children were gazing at True and Paige in mute inquiry.

True cleared his throat again, then said, "We might have a baby someday, yeah.''

Billy nodded, as if a suspicion had been confirmed. "That's what the doctor said.''

"What doctor?"

Billy explained. "At the wedding, I heard the vet,

Dr. Nolan, bet Paige's dad fifty bucks that me and Becca'd have a baby brother by Christmas.''

Paige promised herself she would kick Kathryn's husband's behind the next time she saw him. This was not exactly the subject she wanted to address on her first night with these children.

"Dr. Nolan was just joking, too,'' True told the kids. "And it's not anyone's business but ours if we have a baby.''

Becca's plump features hardened. "Not even me and Billy's business?''

"Of course it's your business, too,'' Paige said quickly. "What your Dad meant is that it's our *family's* business. Isn't that right, True?''

True slipped an arm around Paige's waist and smiled at the kids. "That's exactly right. Our family. Me and Paige and the two of you.''

"What about Aunt Helen?'' Billy asked. "She's our family. Does she get to say when we can have a baby?''

Becca rolled her eyes. "You dummy, Billy. Nobody can just say when somebody else can have a baby. You know how it happens.''

As True reprimanded Becca, Paige felt sorry for poor Billy. He colored, looked confused, then lashed back at his sister. "Dad said we could say when we'd have a baby.'' He glanced at his father. "Didn't you?''

The edges of True's mouth quivered, but Paige was relieved that he suppressed his smile. "That's not exactly right, son.'' He tousled the boy's dark hair.

"What I meant is that we'll all discuss this when the time's right."

"When will that be?" Billy pressed.

"Probably when Paige and I decide we want a baby." This time he smiled at his children. "A baby brother might be nice, don't you think?"

The question brought a smile to Billy's face. He appeared to think a baby might not be so bad.

Not Becca. "No," she said. Simply. Bluntly. "I don't think a baby would be nice at all." Small shoulders held straight and stiff, she stalked from the room before True could react, before Paige could prevent a small, startled gasp.

Billy looked apologetic. He backed toward the door, opened his mouth as if to say something, then just mumbled, "Good night." He scampered after Becca.

In the uncomfortable silence that followed, Paige looked at True. "I think you should go reassure her that we're not having a baby just yet."

To her surprise, True shook his head. "She'll be fine. And when we do want to have a baby, she'll accept it."

Paige gazed at him in dismay. "Aren't you being a little bit overly optimistic, even for you? She seemed upset to me."

"She was just being Becca. She wants everything to be her idea."

"But that's not the way it is."

"Of course not."

"And what happens when we do something she doesn't like?"

"She gets over it."

"Or secretly lets the resentment build."

True frowned. "You're making too much of this."

Turning on her heel, Paige said stubbornly, "If you won't go talk to her, I will."

"Now wait a minute." True caught her by the elbow. "That's not a good move."

"Last night you told me I should trust my judgment about the kids."

"I know, but—"

"But now you're afraid Becca might resent me coming up to talk to her."

"She might," True admitted after a moment's hesitation.

"Then let's go together."

True's jaw tightened. "Would you listen to me on this? We need to just let her alone. Becca doesn't like being smothered. Neither of my kids do."

Paige didn't believe a few reassurances could be construed as smothering. But she recognized the stubborn look on True's face. He thought he knew best where Becca was concerned, and certainly she was his child. Paige, however, couldn't just let this go.

"Let's go up together," she insisted, holding up a hand when True began a protest. "Just to say goodnight. Don't you usually tuck the kids in?"

"They'll be ten years old in two weeks," True reminded her.

"But a lot of things are changing in their world. I think they could do with a little extra attention." Without waiting for True's approval, Paige started toward the door.

With obvious reluctance, True trailed Paige through the kitchen and up the back stairs. She realized as soon as they mounted the last step that she hadn't been on the top floor of this house since she and True were teenagers. She remembered the layout well, however. Four rooms had once opened off the central hall. A small bathroom had been carved from one of those rooms when the house had been modernized, and the leftover space had been converted into a big storage closet, leaving just three large bedrooms.

Again, Paige noted that few improvements had been made to the house over the years. True had admitted himself that his home needed some work. She was glad he was in agreement, since she was going to make those renovations a priority.

But she was pleased to see changes had been made to the twins' front rooms. Billy's room had once been True's and was painted a deep blue, with framed prints and posters celebrating both football and horses, the boy's most fervent passions. Billy's bed was unmade and rumpled, but empty.

Muted voices could be heard coming from the cracked door of the other front bedroom. Those whispers ceased abruptly when True rapped on the door facing. "I think it's past time for bed," he said, pushing open the door.

The room was a sunny yellow, as neat as Billy's room had been messy and featuring a white wicker bookcase with a collection of dolls. Paige was relieved to see the fancy-dressed doll she had given Becca after dinner nestled among the others on the middle shelf. Just above the room's white wainscot-ting was a charming border of hand-painted daisies. Paige wondered if this was Marcie's handiwork. The homey country kitchen was the only other area of the house that seemed to bear an imprint of the woman Paige remembered as pretty and fashionable.

Paige chastised herself for thinking of Marcie. She and True had enough adjustments to make without her starting to compare herself to the twins' mother. Most important was Paige's relationship with these children. She couldn't take their mother's place, but she did want to be an important part of their lives. From the beginning, True had said that was what he wanted, what he believed Billy and Becca needed.

Standing at her desk near a dormer window, Becca was busily sliding books into a backpack, not even glancing up at True and Paige.

Billy, who was seated on the end of a half bed, grumbled, "I'm not sleepy."

True jerked a thumb toward the boy's room. "It's ten o'clock, half an hour past bedtime. You'll be sleepy tomorrow when I try to get you up for school."

With only a bit more fussing, the youngster started toward his room. True promised to be in to say good-night. Paige sent Billy a tentative smile, which he returned with only a small glance toward his sister before leaving.

Becca was standing in front of the dresser mirror, slowly drawing a brush through her long, chestnut hair.

"Bedtime, princess," True said.

She set the brush down with slow, studied care.

With the same sort of deliberate movements, she shed her robe and climbed between yellow-and-blue gingham sheets. All without saying a word.

Paige stuck close to True as he sat down on the edge of Becca's bed. She felt it was important that the two of them present themselves as a team.

True tugged the blanket up to Becca's chin and briefly touched her cheek. "You all right, sweetheart?"

"I'm fine." Her expressionless tone contradicted her words.

Her father seemed satisfied; Paige wasn't. She put her hand on True's shoulder, but spoke to the little girl. "Becca, if there's anything you want to ask us about or say, you can."

"I don't." Becca gave a quick, false smile. "Good night."

Paige ignored the frown True gave her and persevered. "You seemed upset earlier, when we were talking about babies. That's not going to happen right away, and we will talk to you about it before it does. Okay?"

The child's gaze met hers, and for just a moment Paige thought she glimpsed a yearning, a vulnerability that was quickly and efficiently masked by another prim statement. "I understand. And I'm fine. Good night."

True gave her a kiss and a smile before standing. "You sleep tight, now. Me and Paige are glad to be home with you and your brother."

As he crossed the room and snapped off the overhead light, Paige hesitated a moment more beside the little girl's bed. She didn't think a kiss would be welcome, so she settled on a smile before reaching for the bedside lamp.

Becca's head came off the pillow. "Don't."

"She likes a light on," True explained.

His daughter looked at Paige as if challenging her to find fault with that need. But Paige was the least likely person in the world to question her night-light. For she had once been a little girl who had lost her mother too young, who had tried to pretend she was tough and brave and who had slept with a light burning beside her bed even after she moved away from home. For the first time, Paige felt some genuine confidence about trying to establish a bond with this child. She and Becca had at least one thing in common.

"See you in the morning," she said, smiling at Becca once more before joining True in the hall.

"I told you she was okay," he murmured. "You just have to give her some space."

Paige gave a noncommittal reply and followed him into Billy's room. Despite the boy's protests about not being sleepy, he was already so groggy he could barely mumble a good-night.

But the ritual left Paige feeling content as she and True went downstairs. The house was silent except for the sighing of the winter wind around the corners outside. In the fireplace, a log fell into the embers of their evening fire, sending up a shower of sparks. Paige hugged herself, suddenly warmed through and through. She was with *her* husband in *their* home. Dreams were being fulfilled.

Her dream man yawned and rubbed his neck. "Long day, huh?"

She slipped her hand into his, tugging him toward the back hall. "Why don't you get a shower and come to bed?"

His grin full of sexy promise, True paused to check the lock on the porch door and flip off the kitchen lights.

Paige noticed he left a table lamp burning not far from the stairs. "What about that one?"

"I'm leaving it on for Becca."

"She gets up at night?"

He shrugged. "She has. And I'm down here now."

Once they were in the bedroom, Paige turned to True in concern. "Are you upset about Tillie and Helen moving us down here?"

"Not upset, exactly." He lifted and opened his unpacked suitcase on the chest at the foot of the bed.

"I think it was thoughtful of them to do this."

"It'll just take some getting used to for everybody." True plucked his shaving kit from the case and headed for the bathroom.

Paige followed and stood in the doorway, watching him transfer toiletries to the empty medicine chest. Finally, she said, "Don't you feel a little more comfortable being down here?"

His gaze caught hers in the mirror, and True realized what she was getting at. His bringing Paige into the room and the bed he had shared with Marcie, especially when there were other alternatives, would have been the height of insensitivity. Yet he would have done just that if not for his aunt and Tillie. He was suddenly, intensely ashamed of himself.

He closed the chest's mirrored door slowly. "I tell you what I don't like." He looked at Paige. "I don't like that I wasn't the one who thought to move us."

She smiled. "We got married too fast for you to think of everything."

But he had thought of nothing. He had been the one to rush the marriage, but he had spared little thought for their living arrangements. He had figured, selfishly, that Paige would fit herself with ease into the open space in his home. Another miscalculation, he saw now. Just like his assumption that she would become his lover without any preliminary wooing or adjustments. Or that she wouldn't want a wedding. He wondered what other erroneous conclusions he had drawn.

Paige looked concerned. "Is something wrong?"

Afraid to even mention his worries, he put his arms around her and lied, "I was just thinking about all the things I've got to do tomorrow."

"Me, too. I've got to make a dent in this unpacking, then get over to the ranch."

"But you'll be home when the kids get here tomorrow afternoon."

She shrugged. "I'm not sure."

"I'd like you to be."

A tiny line formed between her eyebrows as she gazed up at him. "How come?"

"I just think they like having someone here when they get home."

"Aunt Helen's not leaving until Saturday. I'm sure she will be here."

"Don't you think they should get used to you? She will be gone, and they'll be looking to you."

Paige continued to frown. "I don't know if I can be here every afternoon. And the kids seem very capable of a few hours on their own, especially since there's always someone around the barn or the ranch office."

"It's not the same."

"I think it is."

True realized he was making a big deal about what seemed a small point to Paige. But after only three days of marriage, a lot of his expectations about their union hadn't been met. Now she was balking about a simple request for her to be home when his children returned from a day at school. He wanted Paige here. He thought it was important. And he thought it was a request she should have expected when she agreed to marry him. Hadn't he told her up front that he wanted a mother for his children? Well, in his definition of mother, this was part of the deal.

Stepping back from her, he said, "Will you please be here?"

Maybe she could see that he had drawn a line in the sand. After only a brief hesitation, she said, "I will be here tomorrow afternoon."

"How about after that?"

Her mouth opened, then she closed it, biting her bottom lip. "I'll try if it means so much to you."

"It does." True took a deep breath and let it out slowly. "Now I'm going to get a shower, okay?"

Nodding, Paige left him in the bathroom.

The hot, stinging water cleared some of the tension from True. He realized he had sounded pretty harsh. He wasn't surprised when Paige had nothing to say to him when he returned to the bedroom. In fact, all she did was dart him an angry look.

While he located some boxers and pulled them on, he watched her unpack a suitcase. He wondered if she realized how much her precise, exaggerated movements mirrored Becca's curt bedtime behavior only a half hour ago.

Finally, he said, "I don't want to fight with you, Paige. Not on our first night home."

"Me, neither."

"But I do think it will be good for you to be here with the twins when they get home in the afternoons."

She shook folds out of a nightgown with unnecessary force. "Where will you be when they get home?"

"I've got a ranch to run."

"So do I."

He started a retort, but she cut him off, brown eyes snapping. "Don't you dare. Don't you dare say it's different for me."

That had been exactly what he planned to say, but he changed tactics quickly. He lifted his hands in a conciliatory gesture. "This is not worth a fight."

He could see her struggling with her temper. Self-control won out. "You're right. It isn't worth a fight." At the closet, she reached for a hanger and glanced at him over her shoulder. "Not now, anyway."

It took determination, but he didn't let that make him angry. This just wasn't right. After the strides they had made toward becoming closer, especially last night, she should be in his arms now. Toward that end, he crossed the room and took the hanger out of her hands.

"I'm trying to put some of my things away," Paige told him, still obviously miffed.

He took the gown out of her other hand and tossed it on the bed. "You can do that tomorrow."

"Maybe I want—"

He kissed her before she could complete the sentence, kissed her with all the pent-up frustration he was feeling inside. She resisted, halfheartedly, then gave herself over to his kiss.

"Now," he murmured after a few moments. "What was it you were saying you wanted?"

She kissed him again. "I don't remember."

Turning to the bed, he picked up the gown he now recognized as the one she had worn on their wedding night. "Why don't you go put this on?"

"Why?"

"So that I can take it off."

With a slow, steady smile, she put her arms around his waist. Her hands crept down his back and under the waistband of his boxers, cupping his buttocks. "Only if I can take off your clothes, as well."

"Deal," he murmured before kissing her again.

Somewhere in the middle of that kiss, True heard

the call. Far off, but unmistakable. He had heard it a hundred times before.

"Daddy."

The call was louder the second time, and definitely not his imagination. Paige heard it, too. She stepped away from him before Becca walked in, cheeks wet, rubbing her eyes.

"What's wrong?" True quickly crossed the room to her.

"I'm scared," his daughter sobbed, clutching at his hands. "I can't go to sleep. I keep hearing stuff."

True glanced at Paige. At the pretty, lacy gown she still held. Then down into his daughter's damp, blue eyes. Though he knew it was only the wind she heard, the child was obviously frightened. His choice was clear.

In a quiet voice, Paige said, "You'd better go up and stay with her until she falls asleep. She needs her rest for school tomorrow."

Grateful for Paige's understanding, he said, "I'll be back very soon."

He put on his robe and took Becca up to her room. But even with him sitting beside her bed, she had a difficult time falling asleep. Every time she seemed on the verge of nodding off, she jerked awake again and asked him crazy questions. About her horse, Poppy. About Aunt Helen. Once, she asked for her mother. He hadn't heard her mention Marcie in a long time. Her request twisted True's heart, and when her breath finally evened out, he stayed longer than was necessary, trying to make sure she was well and truly out for the night. It was nearly an hour before he could return to Paige.

He found her asleep.

She looked so peaceful, he decided waking her would be cruel and inhuman. So instead of pleasuring her as he had intended, he had to settle for holding her.

Something he should be getting used to, he thought, frowning ruefully into the darkness.

Chapter Eight

Paige sent a harried look at her wristwatch as she turned her car up the long driveway of the Circle W. It was Thursday. She had been married almost three weeks, and, as had become a habit, she was scrambling to get home in time to meet the twins.

"Damn," she muttered, with another look at her watch. She had been caught up in a telephone conversation with a travel agent when she noticed the time. Since the agent was booking four of the Double M dude cabins for a weekend in May in which they had no other guests scheduled, Paige hadn't the heart to cut the woman off. She had a feeling that wouldn't matter too much to True. He definitely had a thing about her being here for the kids in the afternoon.

She supposed he was right to think the time alone

would force the three of them to get to know one another. Becca and Billy were being nice to her. At least so far.

Paige pulled the car to a stop, flung herself out and raced up the muddy path to the back porch and into the kitchen. A quick glance at the bench just inside the back door revealed the usual pile of coats and sweaters, clear evidence that Becca and Billy were home.

Crossing to the foot of the stairs, she called, "Anybody up there?" At the two answering shouts, she climbed the stairs and paused outside Billy's half-open door. He was just pulling on his favorite worn sweatshirt.

"You been home long?" Paige asked.

He shook his head and started rooting around under his bed. "Just came in. I got lots of homework, but it's warm out and I want to go…" The rest of his sentence was lost as he shoved his body farther under the bed.

Paige had grown used to Billy talking while in motion. He never stopped, and he demanded lots of fuel to keep going. Paige couldn't remember her younger brother consuming the quantities of food Billy needed. Her first attempt to stock the kitchen had been an eye-opener, and it seemed that they ran out of something every other day.

"I know you're starving," she said, once Billy came up for air with one of his work boots. "There should be some of Tillie's pie left from dinner last night, unless your dad finished it at lunch. Or I can fix you some cheese and crackers, or—"

"Paige, come on," Billy interrupted, using what she thought of as his "get real" tone. "I can get my own snack, you know."

They'd had this conversation before. But Paige always offered. The Donna Reed milk-and-cookies-after-school bit seemed to be what True expected of her. She was trying. Most every day it was the same. They had a snack, talked with her for a few minutes about school. Then they disappeared, to their rooms or the barns. On weekdays, they had outside chores involving their horses, which they never seemed to mind. They were supposed to have duties in the house, as well, which as often as not they let slide. On weekends, their chores were all related to the ranch.

True didn't seem too concerned about the tasks they left undone in the house, and Paige wasn't sure where she stood when it came to discipline. Every night that she had gently suggested it was Becca and Billy's turn to do the dishes, True's daughter came up with an excuse, usually schoolwork. Her father hadn't questioned her.

To his credit, he hadn't left the dishes completely to Paige, either.

Unfortunately, the rest of the household duties appeared to rest squarely on her shoulders. She was having a tough time keeping up, especially since the domestic arts were never her claim to fame. She had to admit to a growing resentment and frustration.

Paige had a sneaking suspicion it wouldn't take too much to get Billy to cooperate around the house. He was that kind of easygoing kid. As Helen had pointed out, he had a mischief-making side, but it was usually nothing serious. He had True's athletic ability, and he was breezing through his classes with no problems. He was sunny by nature, and having Paige around seemed to suit him just fine.

Despite his intelligence, however, Billy's sweet disposition allowed Becca to lead him into trouble. Paige had already seen that happen once last week, when they disappeared until well after dark on their horses and no one could find them. It turned out that Becca had been intent on finding a "hidden" canyon that Paige and True had told them they had discovered when they were kids. Problem was, that canyon was a good two-hour ride, not a journey to be undertaken on a cold and quickly darkening February afternoon.

True had been worried sick before he and Paige rode out and found them. Angry, too. But not at the kids. At Paige. Becca claimed she had told Paige where they had headed. Paige, who had been busy returning some calls she hadn't gotten to at the Double M office, couldn't remember the girl saying a word to her about going for a ride. But she might have. Paige had admitted to being distracted. True hadn't cared to hear her explanations.

Knowing the kids had given True a real scare, Paige had gritted her teeth and taken the blame, even though she suspected Becca was fibbing to get out of trouble. No way was Paige going to confront the child. Not without being one hundred percent sure Becca hadn't told her where they were headed. Since then, she had kept a closer eye on the twins. But they had turned ten years old a week ago Sunday. Even True liked to point out they were no longer babies. She didn't want to crowd them so much that they resented her.

It would help if True would sit down and talk to her about all of this.

Fat chance of that, she told herself as she helped Billy locate his other missing boot. The weeks since she and True had returned from their honeymoon had passed with the speed of a storm bearing down on the plains. Like a funnel cloud, everyday life was gobbling up their hours together like so much dust.

First there had been the exhausting task of Paige getting settled in here, and the emotional upheaval of Helen leaving for Lubbock. The twins missed her, and though he would never admit it, Paige knew True did, as well. When he had the time.

A windstorm late last week had wreaked havoc on the roofs of two of the barns. True said their replacement was an expense he had been hoping to put off until fall. He and his hands had been busy trying to do that work, as well as attend to the other ranch work.

Added to that was concern about his stock. Several heifers had calved early, including some stillborns. The veterinarian, Kathryn's husband, Gray, didn't believe there was real cause for alarm. But in the past week, lines of worry and weariness had appeared around True's mouth.

Not the best atmosphere in which to foster some intimacy, Paige thought.

Intimacy.

She almost laughed at the word. Though True had been tenderly amorous a couple of times, not much was happening in their bedroom besides sleep. After their first night home together, she had feared Becca would be a constant interruption, but it was her and True's own hectic pace that was the real culprit. He usually went back to work for several hours after dinner, and she had a dozen or more household tasks to do in the evenings, as well. They were often exhausted.

The nights when she wasn't worn-out, Paige yearned for True's touches. But she always stopped before reaching out to him, feeling unsure and a little shy. If matters between her and True had continued to progress as they had begun, she might be able to act on her impulses. But she felt out of sync with him. Often he seemed distracted and distant.

She admitted to the growing fear that True had some regrets about this marriage. She was afraid he had been unwittingly trying to replace the wife he had lost. But if True wanted her to be anything like Marcie, he was just going to be disappointed. Ever since her first night in this house, Paige had tried to avoid comparing herself to the twins' mother, but insecurities had grown with the awkwardness between her and True.

Billy called out in triumph, claiming Paige's attention once more. Of all places, his missing boot was in the closet where it belonged. He put it on and clambered downstairs in search of food, while Paige chuckled and gathered some of the boy's dirty laundry into a heap that she deposited outside his door.

For a few moments, she stared at the closed door of the room True had shared with his first wife. This was the only room she hadn't explored. And she wasn't now, she told herself firmly. Instead, she called out to Becca.

Her bedroom door was open, but Paige paused and asked permission to come in. Like most little girls, Becca was protective of her private space. From her desk, she gave Paige a subdued welcome as she pushed some papers to the side.

"How was that social studies test?" Paige asked. Last night after dinner, Becca had been obsessing about an upcoming quiz. Billy and Paige had taken turns drilling her with questions, while True did some bookkeeping down in his office.

"Okay" was Becca's uninformative answer.

Knowing the girl's teacher had sent home a note about some recent low marks, Paige added, "Has Miss Turner graded it yet?"

With reluctance, Becca presented one of the papers she had shunted to the side. A red *D* was marked at the top.

"Oh," Paige murmured, trying not to appear too dismayed. A quick glance at the paper revealed Becca had missed some of the very questions she had answered easily last night.

"Billy got an *A*," Becca said, her shoulders slumping.

Though Paige had been careful about displaying too much physical affection, especially with Becca, she couldn't resist hugging the girl now. She felt True tended to lump the children together, expecting that what one could do, the other could as well. But Paige could see a lot of differences between them. She knew Billy's academic prowess was a source of dismay to Becca, and probably another one of the reasons she delighted in getting him in trouble. And surely, the thought of another brother with whom to compete was why Becca had become so upset at the possibility of Paige and True having a baby.

Right now, Becca didn't return Paige's hug, but she didn't resist it, either. She looked miserable, and she was unusually talkative. "Dad's going to say I didn't try."

"But you really studied last night. I told him so." In fact, a discussion about Becca's studying had been the extent of their pillow talk before Paige fell asleep last night.

"It doesn't matter," Becca said. "I don't know why I can't remember this stuff like Billy does."

"Maybe you need some extra help."

Becca shrugged.

"I could come in and talk to Miss Turner about it."

"Do you think Dad would?"

"Why don't you ask him?" Paige suggested, not really too surprised that Becca would prefer her father to handle this.

But the child was reconsidering. "He'll just tell me to get Billy to help me. And to study harder. But that never works."

Paige thought Becca was greatly exaggerating True's insensitivity, but she was disturbed that the little girl was so reluctant to reveal any sort of weakness to her father. Helen had said Becca was competing with her brother for True's attention and affection.

True didn't love his son more, but he did tend to approve most vocally of the schoolwork and sports that came easily to Billy. Both twins were excellent riders, but Billy was the real daredevil. He got True's eye more easily. Paige, however, had noticed the horses responded more to Becca's easy touch and soothing voice. Certainly, the child loved those horses, especially Poppy, the expectant mare. Becca had big plans for training Poppy's son or daughter. Paige suspected she would do a wonderful job.

But it was Becca's skills in the classroom that were most important right now, and she didn't want her father to know about this test score. "Please don't tell him about this," she implored Paige. "I'll do better on the next one. I promise I will."

Becca was so upset that Paige had to agree. If nothing else, this conversation showed her overtures toward True's daughter were paying off. She would find some way of getting the child some help at school without telling True about this particular test.

"All right," Paige said, handing the quiz back to Becca. "Let's forget this for now." She looked toward the window, where bright sunlight was streaming inside. After a week of winter, it was warm outside, just as Billy had pointed out earlier. The thought of staying inside and cooking dinner or doing any of the copious piles of laundry made Paige want to scream. Hell, she had never been any good at either of those things. She had this terrible feeling True thought that had changed, but she didn't care right now.

"Come on," she said to Becca. "Let's get Billy and go for a ride."

"I've got a lot of homework," the child said uncertainly.

"I'll help you later," Paige promised, heading for the door. "Get your boots on." Then she left, calling for Billy.

The sight of Paige and the twins riding at a full gallop across the flat land south of the house put a funny hitch in True's gut.

They were racing, with Billy out front on the palomino daughter of True's own favorite mount. But Paige and Becca were coming on strong on a set of matching roans.

Paige still rode the same as always, True thought. Like she was molded to the horse. With just an edge of recklessness.

She showed that now, surging forward to take the lead from Billy and leaving both twins in the dust. She raced by True, waving her hat and whooping it up. The twins galloped on, obviously deciding on a contest of their own, but Paige pulled up and trotted back to where True sat on Goldie.

The hitch in his gut turned to blatant yearning. There was a light in her face, a beauty that had nothing to do with looks and everything to do with spirit. She stirred something wild in him, the very feelings he had been holding in check ever since their honeymoon. Her laughter was so bright, so uninhibited, that he responded in kind.

At the same time, he realized he couldn't remember smiling, much less laughing, in the past week. He had been so damn busy, so focused on the ranch, that he had been neglecting his family, especially his new wife. All the plans he had made for her slow, sweet seduction had turned into wishful thinking.

What was it Aunt Helen had said to him before he married Paige? That he had tunnel vision. It was the same thing as being single-minded, something he used to think was an asset. He was beginning to see why his aunt had called that quality a fault, as well.

He needed to get his priorities in order, True decided as Paige drew near. A man married to a woman this alive needed to pay some attention to her. Close attention.

"Where's the fire?" he asked by way of greeting.

"It's in my belly," she claimed. She threw her head back and took in a gulp of air. "It feels so good out here, I could almost believe it's April or May instead of February."

"Now you've jinxed the weather. Every time someone in West Texas says spring has come this early, we end up getting a blizzard."

"I refuse to believe that could happen." She sent him an arch look. "You're too much of a downer for my taste, Mr. Whitman. I think you need to shake some of your cobwebs loose."

"What do you have in mind?"

"A race to the creek?"

The challenge was as old as their friendship. How

many times had they raced over this field? His father used to say True wasted the best hours of the workday racing Paige McMullen. He should heed his father's remembered advice, decline Paige's challenge and get on over to the far corner of the ranch, where a fence hadn't been checked since last week's storm. But that held little appeal when he considered giving Goldie her head and Paige a run for her money to the creek.

Duty-bound, however, he hesitated. He reached over and patted Paige's mount on the neck. "You've already given this horse a workout. She's not up for another race."

"Penny's a stouthearted gal." Paige sent him a pity-filled glance. "I guess it's you and Goldie who aren't up to the challenge. I guess you're getting old."

"Not hardly."

"Sure is disappointing to see you fade this young."

Her deliberate baiting gave True an idea. "I'll race," he said, voice heavy with suggestion. "But only if the winner gets to choose his prize."

"Yes, *she* does," Paige agreed. A wicked intent, which pleased True to no end, gleamed in her eyes. "Any prize at all."

Becca and Billy rode up just as they aligned their horses. Excited at the announcement of a race between Paige and their father, the twins counted down and started the contest with a shout. Just like old times, Paige and True were off.

And just like always, she hung back at first, letting True get cocky. Then she moved in for the kill, nosing past him at the thicket that marked the edge of the creek bed. She had half a length on him by the time they reached their goal.

Finally slowing her horse to a gentle canter at the edge of the shallow creek, Paige turned with a shouted, "Yee-haw!" True just shook his head, accepting defeat.

"When will you learn, Whitman?" she demanded teasingly. "You've got to save your strength for that last surge."

He rode up beside her. "You can still ride with the best of them, Slim. Nobody'd know you spent all that time out on the coast."

"You think I didn't ride out there? I knew I'd die if I didn't get on horseback at least twice a week." She patted Penny before flashing him another brilliant smile. "But it is nicer to be riding at home on a good Texas horse."

True reached out and covered her gloved hands with one of his own. "I, for one, sure am glad you got wise and came home."

"Are you?" Paige murmured, the sudden seriousness in her tone taking True by surprise.

"Of course."

She glanced down at her saddle's pommel, where their hands rested. "I've been thinking...well, worrying is more like it." The muscles worked visibly in her throat before she continued. "We haven't had much time for each other."

Frowning at the note of genuine hurt in her tone, he said, "I was just thinking about that a few minutes ago. We haven't gotten off to the kind of start I wanted. Too much has been going on. But we can manage better than we have been.''

Paige slanted a look back up at him, sadness gone, replaced by flirtatious suggestions. ''What are you going to do about it?''

''Well…'' True allowed Goldie to dance closer to Paige's horse as he leaned in close for a kiss. Settling back, he murmured, ''For starters, you could let this loser claim a prize.''

''Even if it's you I want as my prize?''

Her breathless question hung in the air between them before the twins came riding up. Keeping up any sort of romantic dialogue was impossible with two ten-year-olds begging for attention, so True didn't try.

But as she turned Penny toward home, Paige sent him a look. All female. Completely seductive. That glance lifted True's every care. He realized he had been waiting for a glance like that, some encouragement from Paige. Since the night he had invaded her bath and promised to let her set the pace of their sexual relationship, he had been uncertain of what she wanted the next move to be. They had come together since, with similar intimacy. But he always stopped. She always let him. He read a change in her now. At least he hoped he was reading her right.

Suddenly eager to be home, True herded his protesting children after Paige.

Over grooming chores in the stable, his gaze met hers and lingered again and again. Around them, Becca and Billy chattered away, not seeming to care that they got only grunts from their father and little more from Paige. True's whole being seemed focused on her.

On his way to store his saddle, his arm "accidentally" brushed against her breasts. His hands "just happened" to graze her behind. And in a corner of the tack room, while their chaperones were busy elsewhere, his lips "somehow" found their way to her very willing mouth.

"I sure hope those heathens of mine go to bed early," he whispered before she slipped out of his arms.

Paige sent him a look full of feminine mystery. Anticipation was singing through his veins.

Dinner, one of Paige's less than spectacular casseroles, took forever.

Homework was interminable.

The bedtime ritual begun on their first night home with the children dragged on and on and on. After Becca had been tucked in, Paige said her good-nights to Billy and left True to listen as patiently as he could and give his son some guidance about a squabble with a friend at school. He could only hope he gave the boy some sort of intelligible answer.

Whatever he said, it seemed to be a long time before True could leave Billy to his slumbers and slip out into the darkened hall. He was startled to find Paige still upstairs. She was standing, nearly invisible in her black jeans and sweater, in the open doorway of the room he had once shared with Marcie.

He eased up behind her, whispering, "What are you doing?"

She jumped and glanced around. "I'm sorry. What did you say?"

"Are you looking for something?"

She hesitated for just a moment, then stepped out in the hall, closing the door behind her. She put her arms around him. "I was waiting for you. Take me down to bed."

"Gladly, ma'am," he drawled. "You want to be carried?"

"Well, I didn't want to say anything, but you never have carried me over any thresholds. I'm feeling slighted."

He took her hand. "We'll do something about that right now."

Downstairs, he led her over to the porch door and opened it to a chilly breeze. On the porch, he swept her up in his arms and kissed her as he carried her back into the kitchen.

"That's much better, Mr. Whitman."

"Sorry it took so long, *Mrs.* Whitman."

He carried her on into their bedroom. The lights were dim. The rumpled sheets of the bed left unmade this morning were welcoming.

True set Paige on her feet and kissed her again, wisely not giving her time to think. This afternoon, as she had ridden across the ranch with the wind in her face, Paige had decided she did too much thinking. She needed to act, to follow her heart and her instincts about True and his children. Out there in the false-spring sunshine, she had decided to become True's wife in every sense of the word.

She had done one thing more, as well. Upstairs,

while she had waited for True, she had gone into his and Marcie's room. She had gazed at the frilly curtains and the hand-embroidered bedspread. That room was exactly right for the woman Paige remembered Marcie to be. And Paige was nothing like Marcie, the woman True had loved. If she tried to imitate her, as Paige halfway feared True had been hoping she could, then she was doomed to failure and him to disappointment.

Fact was, however, he had married Paige. He said he wanted her. Surely the closeness of making love with him would smooth the way in the other areas of their life. She had to accept what True could give, just as he had to take her as she was, as well. This was a marriage of convenience, not a loving courtship. But it was time they set one aspect of this marriage on a traditional path.

Just as deliberately as she had shut the door to the room upstairs, Paige closed her mind to everything but sensation. True's hands were in her hair. His lips were at her throat, on her mouth. He cast aside her sweater and bra, cupped her breasts for a moment and made short work of his own clothes and her jeans. She was clad only in white cotton panties when he tumbled them both to the bed.

"If I had been thinking far enough ahead, these would have been silk," Paige murmured, touching her practical bikini briefs.

"What does it matter?" True hooked a finger in the stretchy knit. "They're coming off."

"Thank goodness." She lifted her hips off the bed to aid in the progress.

Laughing, he pushed her panties down her legs and flung them away. He loomed over her, shoulders broad and tightly muscled, his work-worn hands sliding slowly up her thighs, over her stomach and midriff to her breasts. His voice was husky. "I hope you're ready for your prize, Slim."

"Judge for yourself." As bold as she had been hesitant for the past few weeks, she took his hand and guided it between her legs. She was damp and warm. More than ready for him.

But he took his time and touched her everywhere. With his hands and his mouth. Tongue probing. Voice murmuring his naughty, sexy approval of her body and its reaction to his. Beard rasping not unpleasantly against her breasts. Her ribs. Her inner thighs. Between them. One lave of his tongue brought her to a shatteringly intense climax.

While her world was spinning, he left her and came back from the bathroom with several small, square packets. By the soft light of the bedside lamp, she watched his deft movements. They smiled at each other as he came back to her.

Silent, her gaze remained steady on his as he slipped his hands beneath her knees, tenderly spreading her legs. He fit his hips to hers, his hard shaft probing her wet, eager cleft. True guided the pulsing tip up and then down, stroking that most sensitive seam of her body. At that moment, Paige couldn't imagine why she had let the past few weeks go to waste. She wanted him as badly as she wanted to draw her next breath. So she tilted her pelvis upward. Met him. Took him in.

And True took her.

There was one uncomfortable moment. Then her body adjusted to his, closing around him, glorying in his every hot, eager thrust.

He came quickly, or at least he said it was fast. Too fast.

"Was it?" Paige tightened her legs around him and savored the last, delicious tremors of his orgasm. Unworried about the quickness of the moment, she was lost in the excitement of his possession, in a feeling of oneness that took her by surprise. She had loved True for so long. She had waited for this, for him to be the one who claimed her innocence. She wasn't one bit disappointed.

He took his weight off her, withdrawing from her body and settling alongside her. All concern, he whispered, "Did I hurt you?"

"Only in all kinds of good ways."

He chuckled low in his throat, the sound as masculine and arousing as his most intimate kiss. "You're something else, Slim."

Feathering a hand through his close-cropped hair, she said, "I hope I'm something you like."

He kissed her neck, then nuzzled at one breast. "Very much."

Her next words just sort of tumbled out. "You know I love you, don't you?"

True went still. He rested his forehead against her shoulder.

She couldn't seem to shut up. "I've always loved you. Even before I knew I loved you, I did. I used to dream about marrying you and having your babies.

About us joining these two ranches and working together.'' She swallowed around the knot that had grown in her throat. Damned, unwanted tears burned in her eyes. She wished he would say something. Anything. Even if he told her to hush.

But he didn't. He just drew away and looked at her, his reactions hidden by the dim light and the inscrutable set of his jaw.

She blundered on, ''I do love you. That's why I married you, True. Because it's all I ever really wanted. And in my own way, I'm trying to be the wife you need.''

His reply was a kiss. A deep kiss. Bordering on raw. This kiss didn't speak to her of love, but it showed her his passion. Low against her hip, his sex stirred, hard and quickly heavy. For her. Just for her. Without shame, Paige knew she would be content with this if it was all he could offer.

Her tears cleared as the kiss continued. It was stupid to be sad at a moment that was so good. Maybe she shouldn't have told True how much she loved him. But she was trying to keep the promise she had made herself earlier. She was following her heart and her instincts. She could only be the person that she was. Pretenses had never been her style. And loving William True Whitman had been part of her for as long as she could remember. He might as well accept it now, the same as he had better accept all her other shortcomings and gifts.

Drawing away from his kiss, she reached down to caress his aroused manhood. ''My goodness, it seems that race this afternoon finally taught you something.''

''What?''

''To save your strength for the last surge.''

His grin reappeared, and she was pleased to see her momentary lapse of emotional intensity hadn't destroyed the fragile beauty of this night. She didn't want him guilty because he didn't love her.

Indeed, guilt seemed the last thing on True's mind right now. Efficiently, he disposed of the evidence of their first lovemaking and reached for another of the square packets he had placed on the bedside table.

He winked at Paige as he broke open the seal. ''Better get ready, Slim. I'm saddling up.''

Desire uncurled in her belly as she took in the taut lines of his torso. This was the man of all her fantasies—with strong legs, a broad chest and arms corded with muscles. Suddenly eager, she sat up and lent a hand to his protective measures. Then she pushed him down on the bed and straddled his hips.

''Sure you're up for another race?'' True teased.

Following her instincts, she lowered herself onto his thickened shaft. He stretched her, filled her. In ways he hadn't only minutes ago. This was something she could learn to like. A lot.

As she began to move, she said, ''Don't you know? I'm a stouthearted Texas gal, always ready for a ride.''

The only reply True could make was an enthusiastic, though slightly breathless, ''Yee-haw!''

Chapter Nine

True had never been particularly fond of surprises. He wanted stability, sameness, security. Those qualities were part of what he had missed about not being married. He liked everything steady and smooth. He had imagined such a life with Paige.

Clearly, he could remember that night at her father's house, when he had watched her serve coffee and pie, as sweet and tame and content as a house cat.

Who could have guessed she would turn out to be a wildcat?

Helen had tried to warn him, he recalled. She had tried to remind him of Paige's spirited nature and penchant for unpredictability when they were kids. But True hadn't listened.

And one right after another, Paige had been dropping surprises on him. She was nothing like the wife he had imagined for himself.

There were some benefits, however. Especially in bed.

As he guided his truck over a rough ranch road, True peered through the cold, late-afternoon rain and smiled. The three and a half weeks since he and Paige had become lovers had turned into the most sexually adventurous experience of his life.

He couldn't seem to get enough of her. Or she of him. In all sorts of ways. Her initial shyness had evaporated, replaced by an inventiveness that stole his breath. Just this morning, after the kids were off to the bus and he should have been hard at work, she had induced him back to bed. She had stroked him, teased him, taken him into her hands and her mouth before claiming his release.

Remembering her gentle laugh, her eager touch and the sweet welcome of her body, True shifted uncomfortably in his seat. Without question, he wanted her with an intensity that continued to catch him off guard.

But outside the bedroom, some of her surprises hadn't been so welcome.

She couldn't cook worth a damn.

She would rather muck out a horse's stall than clean house.

She had a temper as unpredictable as lightning.

And she liked to tell him she loved him.

True wasn't sure why this last point bothered him so much. That first night they had made love, Paige's confession of love hadn't been a total shock. He had known how deep her feelings for him ran since the day she had picked out her wedding dress. But knowing how she felt and hearing her say it were two separate things. He certainly didn't anticipate the way she kept telling him. In notes left on the bathroom mirror. In the morning when they parted. In front of the kids.

Having grown up in and out of Paige's home, True was well aware that the McMullen clan were a more demonstrative bunch than his own family. Hell, he could count on one hand the times his father had told him he loved him. The same went for Helen. True had followed that tradition with Marcie and the kids.

Not Paige. She offered her heart. Often.

The children were warming to her easy affection. Billy, especially. She felt the boy was missing Aunt Helen, so she called the older woman and let him talk to her several nights a week. Paige had hit upon the idea of Billy keeping a journal to send to her, as well. True had imagined his son would tire of that within days, but Billy wrote faithfully every night. This morning, he had given the first week's installment to Paige to mail to Helen. Then he had hugged her goodbye. When he was gone, Paige had cried, overjoyed that True's son was coming to care for her.

Becca would probably not be giving Paige such open displays of sentiment anytime soon. Many afternoons, however, Paige could be found with her down at the stables, talking quietly as they walked Poppy, the mare who was due to foal anytime. True wasn't sure if it was due to Paige's influence, but there seemed to be fewer fights between the twins and less getting into mischief.

True might have been able to sit back, content with the way Paige was fitting into his children's lives. But sitting back didn't seem to be allowed in Paige's world. Dimly, he remembered thinking marriage would relieve him of some of the day-to-day responsibilities of child-rearing. Paige had other ideas.

She dragged him into every decision about the children. Their schoolwork. Their clothes. And most especially, their feelings.

These days, there was a lot of talk in his house about feelings.

And that was at the heart of True's growing uneasiness. Because he was uncomfortable with Paige's offers of unqualified love, he struck out at her for the little things that bothered him—the cooking and housework and such.

Last night, they had argued about her spending every spare minute over at the Double M. True knew her father wasn't up to speed yet, and Paige had confessed some of the financial worries facing her family ranch. They needed a solid spring and summer tourist season, and she was working hard to attract new business and lure back some of their old clientele who had drifted away these past few years. She was making major repairs to the dude cabins and planning new entertainment and programs.

At the same time, she and the new foreman were trying to upgrade the ranching side of the spread. They were facing the same worries about stock and weather that True was. More than most, he understood the fiscal juggling Paige was going through.

Yet last night, True had looked around at piles of

laundry, unmade beds and dirty dishes and asked Paige to spend more time at home. Predictably, she got mad as fire and told him to get over it.

True had gotten angry, as well, and went down to the office. When he came back, she still wanted to fight. He made love to her, instead.

He liked arguments only a little less than surprises. He avoided them in every way he could. Converting his anger into sexual energy was the most pleasant way to practice such avoidance.

Something told him, however, that Paige wouldn't put up with that forever.

Driving past the barns, True brought the truck to a stop near the house, noting two strange cars parked beside Paige's little blue Honda. He got out and turned up his collar as he hurried toward the back porch. The rain was colder, and would probably turn to ice before morning. Not good news for his breeding stock that had been calving steadily throughout the warm, false-spring weather of the past two weeks.

True was trying not to worry, but earlier in the month he had lost more calves than he planned for. With the unexpected expense of new roofs on the barns, he was hitting the margins of his operating expenses a little too close for comfort. He was going to have to shelve plans for renovating the house for a few months. Since Paige had spent last weekend collecting paint samples and making plans, he wasn't looking forward to telling her they would have to wait.

In the house True found Paige, her friend Kathryn and another woman he didn't recognize sitting around the kitchen table drinking coffee. Paige got up to help him out of his wet outerwear. She explained the children were down at the barn before she introduced Jenny, a friend of Kathryn's.

At the counter, Paige poured him some coffee and the women asked him about the weather. True warmed his hands on the mug and eyed Kathryn's greatly rounded belly. She had to be close to term. "It's getting mean out there. Gray won't like you being out in this. Not with that baby coming any day now."

"Yes, Gray will be livid if he finds me gone," Kathryn agreed as she stood. "You would think a veterinarian wouldn't worry so much about a simple little baby like we're having."

Personally, True thought he would lock Paige in the house if she dared come out in weather like this while she was expecting. He said as much after Kathryn and her friend had left.

One hip leaning against the counter where he refilled his mug for a second time, Paige laughed. "I would like to see you try to lock me up."

"How about if we were locked up together?"

She sent a glance toward the staircase. "Good idea. Let's lock ourselves in our room now, while the kids are occupied."

"It's too close to dinnertime. Billy'd bust us for sure."

Paige gave a long, dramatic sigh and kissed him. "I guess we'll just have to wait, won't we?"

He nuzzled her neck. "You're wearing me out, Slim."

"You like it."

"Absolutely."

"It would be nice if we had more time for each other, wouldn't it?"

A discussion of more time together as a couple and as a family had been the start of last night's argument. True drew back, not eager to tread that path again.

But Paige wasn't. "After our argument last night, I did some thinking about the way things are going around here."

He was silent, almost afraid to hear what she was about to say.

She took a deep breath. "I've hired Jenny, the woman you just met, to help us out."

True hesitated, not sure what she meant.

Rushing on, Paige explained, "She's going to do some cleaning, laundry and some cooking, too. Kathryn says she's a fabulous cook and she's a wonderful, honest person and she needs the work."

"Then why doesn't Kathryn hire her?" True interjected tightly.

A defiant gleam lit Paige's eyes. "Because I need her more. This spring and summer Jenny will be working for us over at the Double M on Tuesdays and Fridays, but she's coming in here on the other weekdays starting this Monday."

"You've got to be kidding."

Paige's tone was firm. "We need her, True. I simply can't keep up with everything around here."

"We can't afford a cleaning lady."

"I'm paying."

"No, you're not."

"Don't start that chauvinistic, big Texas male stuff with me," Paige retorted. "Jenny's help is something I want, so I don't see why I can't pay for her. I have savings, and I make a salary from the ranch, you know. I can afford to pay her."

He didn't care. Maybe it made no sense that he didn't care, but the idea of hiring someone to come in and clean his home and wash his clothes hit True all wrong. He and his family had never been the kind of people who hired cleaning ladies. Hell, it hadn't been until True was married and the ranch operation began to grow that his father had consented to hiring more than one ranch hand. Whitmans took care of their own, and that included their own possessions.

"We don't need help," he told Paige, with a firmness he hoped she would take for finality. "There are two adults and two children here to keep this household running."

"But you don't have time to do more than you do now and neither do I."

"We just need to get organized."

Temper was showing in Paige's features. "You're acting like a jerk, you know."

He set his coffee mug down so quickly that liquid splashed over the rim. "What do you mean by that?"

"I know you expected me to take over this house and run it like Helen and…" She paused, swallowed, then added, "Like Helen and Marcie did."

His denial was swift and hot. "I've never said that to you. I've never compared you to anyone."

"You didn't have to say anything," she retorted.

"All you had to do was walk in and look around this mess a few times and give me one of your looks."

"My looks?"

"The one that says, 'God, Paige, what kind of bomb blew up here in the kitchen?'"

He wasn't about to admit she was right. "I don't do that."

"Yes, you do. You did last night before you started in on me working late."

"I didn't start in on you."

"You did so." Her voice rose, much as it had last night when he had tried to have a calm conversation with her about her hours at the Double M.

True clenched his fists at his sides, struggling not to give in to his anger. "All I did was try to talk to you last night. You're the one who blew up and started an argument."

"No, you never start arguments. You just walk away from them."

There was no avoiding the fury that took over him at her challenging words. "What do you mean, I walk away?"

Paige wasn't backing down. She rarely did. "Every time any discussion starts to get too intense, you go down to the office or the barn or out to check the stock."

"I have work to do."

"If you didn't, you'd make something up," Paige claimed, two angry dots of color glowing on her cheeks. "You do everything you can to avoid confronting some of the issues we need to resolve. You even make love to keep from talking about them."

Though her accusations struck a chord of truth, he didn't like hearing it from her. His eyes narrowed and his voice deepened to sarcasm. "I didn't know you resented my making love to you so often. I'll remember that and try to do better." Turning on his heel, he started toward the door.

"There you go," Paige claimed. "Walking away again."

He stopped, his hand on the doorknob, not looking back. "I think it might be better if we continued this later, when we both calm down."

"I don't want to calm down." The heated declaration was followed by an object whizzing through the air.

True jumped as a coffee mug shattered against the wall, well past any danger of striking him, but still too close for comfort. He jerked around to face Paige. "That's good. Go ahead and be childish."

Brown eyes blazing, Paige said, "You're childish, too. Childish and blind. You've got this set little way in which your world is supposed to work. If it doesn't, you just put your head down and keep on going, pretending that all is well."

Her words were uncomfortably close to those his aunt had used to describe him the day Paige agreed to marry him. The idea of the two of them comparing notes on him made True see red. "If you've been listening to Aunt Helen—"

"I should have listened and believed her when she said you can be pigheaded, arrogant and selfish."

"With a recommendation like that, I'm surprised you married me." He headed toward the door again.

No matter what Paige said about him walking away, he was intent on getting out of here before he completely lost his grip.

"You know why I married you." This time it was the quiet huskiness of her voice that brought him to a halt.

True raked a hand through his hair, but didn't turn. He was waiting for her to say she loved him. He was surprised when the words didn't come. And maybe a little disappointed. This last emotion struck him hard, left him immobile. Shouldn't he be relieved that she wasn't pushing her love at him in her usual way?

While he hesitated, Paige came up behind him, slipping her arms around his waist. Her voice was fiercely tender. "Why are we fighting like this?"

"You tell me," he said, not relaxing at her touch. Just as he couldn't give in to his anger as quickly as she, he couldn't let go of it so easily, either.

She continued, "Seems to me you got all hot and bothered because I don't want to spend my time on housework."

When she put it that way, he sounded petty and small-minded, and he hated that she called him on it.

"I'm sorry I can't be Mrs. Superhousewife," she added.

That made him face her. "I didn't ask you to be."

She held up a hand. "Let's not go through that again."

"I'd just as soon not go through any of this any longer."

But that wasn't what Paige had in mind. Her jaw

was set at the determined angle he was getting used to. "I've hired Jenny, and I'm paying her."

"No matter how I feel about it?"

Paige's sigh was long-suffering. "I don't see why you have to make this into a federal case. With her help, instead of me spending half of the evenings on housework, I can be with you. Or with Becca and Billy."

"But what about the message you send them by hiring Jenny?"

A line appeared between her eyebrows. "Message?"

"If you don't want to do something, just find someone who will and write them a check."

"You're being absurd."

"And you grew up different than I did, different from the way I want my children raised."

Her rage exploded again. "Don't go throwing around that nonsense about my family having money. My father always gave me responsibilities and held me accountable for them. From what I've seen, that's a little bit more than you've done with your kids."

He flexed his jaw, stepping closer to her. "Just what in the hell do you mean by that?"

Her eyes widened and he could see her swallow, but she stood her ground. "I think you could be more consistent with Becca and Billy."

"In what way?"

"It seems to me they manage to get out of whatever they want without too much trouble."

"That's something you ought to admire."

"Oh, for pity's sake. There's no talking reasonably

to you, is there?'' With a gesture of disgust, Paige went down the back hall and retrieved a broom and dustpan from a closet.

His intention to escape forgotten, True waited, frowning, for her to return. ''What is it you think I'm doing so wrong with my kids?''

Movements jerky, Paige started sweeping the fragments of the mug into the dustpan. ''I think you had the right idea a minute ago when you started to leave. We're only going to argue more if we keep on.''

True wasn't budging until she told him what he was doing with his kids that had her so hot under the collar. ''I love my children. I'd give my life for them.''

''Love isn't the issue.''

''What is?''

''Attention, maybe.''

His hands went to his hips. ''Stop talking in shorthand and tell me what that means.''

Paige dumped the broken cup in the trash, then faced him, still clutching the broom. ''It's exactly what I was telling you before. You make up your mind about something and that's it, end of story. Even if things start going wrong, you cling to whatever notion you've concocted. You even ignore the obvious.''

''And how does that relate to my son and daughter?''

''Think about Becca. Do you ever talk to her about why she sleeps with that light on?''

''I assume she's afraid of the dark.''

''But do you *know?*''

"No, but—"

"And do you notice, really notice, how hard she tries to keep up with Billy in school?"

"She's every bit as smart as he is."

Paige paused. "Have you considered that maybe she's not?"

"That's nonsense," True exploded. "She's just not as disciplined with her studies."

"Her teacher says she needs some extra help getting her attention focused." Nervously, Paige cleared her throat. "She suggested some sessions with a counselor."

"How do you know that?"

"Because I went to the school today."

"And why didn't you tell me?"

"I haven't had a chance."

"I could have gone to the school with you."

"Becca doesn't want you to think she's not as smart as Billy. She wants you to be proud of her."

True couldn't believe what he was hearing. The idea that he could have neglected or hurt his daughter was like a bucket of ice to his face. "I am proud of her. How could she think I'm not proud?"

Biting her lip, Paige moved toward him. "True, I'm not saying you're a bad father."

He shrugged away from her touch. "Sounds that way to me."

"But you're not," she insisted. "It's just that for some reason Becca needs more of your attention than you've been giving her. Maybe she has felt Marcie's loss more than Billy. Maybe she could tell he was Helen's favorite—"

"Aunt Helen didn't have a favorite," True interrupted.

Paige disagreed. "I think she did, and I think Becca was very aware of it."

"How do you know all this?" he demanded, throat raw with emotion. "How can you possibly know all this about my daughter?"

"I've just been trying to listen to her, to really pay attention to how she acts and what she says. I figured that was the only way I could understand her or hope to get close to her. You and Helen both told me that Becca is deep, that she needs her space and she likes to work through things on her own. You're right, but..." Paige paused, looking at him uncertainly again.

"But what?"

"I don't happen to think little girls who lose their mothers should be given so much space."

"And what qualifies you as an expert?"

Her deep, steady gaze reminded him of how very much Paige had in common with his daughter.

He drew in a long, steadying breath, let it out. "I'm sorry."

Expression miserable, she nodded.

Then they just looked at each other.

True broke the silence. "What do you want me to do?"

For some reason, that made Paige furious. She whirled around, muttering something or the other about men being blind, needing to be led and being full of something Tillie would definitely not approve of her mentioning. She stomped to the closet and threw in the broom and pan.

Voice raised in irritation, True demanded, "Now what's wrong? What did I say?"

Paige jerked her coat off the rack near the back door and shook her head. "If you don't know..."

He was rapidly losing his cool again. "I don't know, and I don't understand you."

"The feeling's mutual," she shouted as she wrenched open the door.

Becca and Billy were standing on the porch, jaws slackened and eyes big. Obviously they had heard the shouting.

Paige slowed long enough to give them a smile. "You and your dad are on your own tonight, kids. Have fun." She would let True handle their questions.

She didn't pause to look back as she dashed through the rain to her car.

A few hours later the rain was still falling. It beat against the study windows at the Double M. Every now and then, Paige thought she detected the sound of ice pellets mixing in the downpour. Tillie kept reminding her the roads could freeze up in no time at all, but still Paige lingered in a favorite chair by the fire, not eager to go home.

Home. Funny how the word could take on a whole new meaning in only a few months. Home now meant True and the kids.

Paige took a long sip of hot chocolate and stared into the flames leaping behind a mesh fire screen. She wondered what True had found to cook for dinner.

Or if he was worried about her. Seemed like he would call if he was.

"Must have been some kind of fight." Tillie's crisp tone penetrated Paige's wall of misery.

"Must have," Rex agreed, a thread of amusement in his tone.

Paige skewered them both with a look. They were obviously fishing for details about why she had shown up on their doorstep in wet clothes and a foul mood. She had to give them credit, though, for waiting this long to pry the information out of her.

She wasn't so sure she wanted to share the details. "What do you hear from Jarrett?" she asked, referring to her younger brother.

Rex grunted and Tillie clucked.

"Must be bad," Paige prompted.

"He says his grades are the pits," her father reported, shifting in his easy chair. "I don't know what to think about the boy. He doesn't want to ranch, always planned to be a doctor, but now..." Rex shrugged. "You were easier to raise, Paige. Never gave me any trouble."

Not looking up from her knitting, Tillie added, "No trouble is right. Except when she almost wasted away, wanting True Whitman."

Paige uncurled from her chair. "I did no such thing."

But her father chuckled. "You were awful upset when True married Marcie."

"You knew all about that?" Paige asked, sending Tillie a furious glance.

"Don't be looking at me that way," the woman

retorted. "I didn't have to tell your father anything. He could see how you felt."

Rex's gaze was tender on Paige. "I hurt for you, daughter, seeing the way you cared for True. But I knew there was no solution. Even though I knew you wanted to be here, and lord knows, I wanted you here, I encouraged you to move away."

For the first time, Paige realized her father's support of her staying away all these years had involved some sacrifice on his part. She got up, crossed the room and perched on the arm of his chair. It was so good to see him looking well. There was color in his cheeks and a light in his eyes. These days, he was walking with his cane most of the time. His wheelchair sat largely unused in a corner of his room. He might never be the same, but he was stronger every day. She treasured the time she was spending with him.

Draping her arm lightly around his shoulders, she said, "I'd have come home anytime you asked, you know."

He patted her hand. "Of course you would have. You always looked so sad on the last day of a visit."

"Land sakes," Tillie muttered in her practical way. "What's the use in going over all of that? She's home now. Home and married to True." A gust of wind sent rain hard against the window, and the older woman arched one thin eyebrow. "Seems to me you'd be wanting to get home to him, Paige."

"I'm mad at him," Paige said, deciding to confess all.

Tillie set aside her knitting, all ears. "What about?"

"Everything."

Rex took her hand again. "Could you break it down a little more than that?"

"There are a lot of things about him that I didn't know and didn't expect."

For some reason that statement caused her father and Tillie to exchange a knowing look.

Paige studied them with suspicion. "All right. What was that all about?"

"I was worried about what you expected out of True," Tillie explained.

"And I agreed with her," Rex added.

"Why?"

"Good heavens, child." Tillie rolled her eyes. "You were so crazy in love with True when you left here that you couldn't see him for what he was."

"I saw him just fine," Paige retorted. "But in all these years since I left, he has changed."

Tillie sniffed. "True Whitman hasn't changed one lick since he was a boy. People don't change."

"He has," Paige insisted. "I don't remember him being this mule-headed and blind."

"Sounds like the True I've always known," Tillie murmured.

Calmly, her father said, "Paige, dear, you're not the first person to fall blindly in love with someone, only to wake up and realize they're not perfect."

"I'm not asking for perfection. I'm certainly not perfect, either."

Tillie made a soft sound of agreement, earning another of Paige's glares.

Rex laughed again, looking at Paige. "What is it you want from True?"

"I want—" Paige cut off her words abruptly. She had been about to say she wanted True's love. But that wasn't something she could share with her father or Tillie. She and True were married; they were supposed to be in love. They had stood in this house in front of family and friends and promised to love and honor each other. But True hadn't promised Paige the sort of love she wanted, and she had no right to ask for it.

Her father and Tillie were looking at her expectantly, waiting for her to say something. So instead of the lack of love, she focused instead on the other quality she had found most wanting in True these past few weeks. "I want him to accept me, just the way I am."

"Tall order," her father said, shaking his head. "Accepting each other, warts and all, is one of the toughest parts of marriage."

"Don't mind marriage," Tillie put in. "Accepting each other is the hardest thing any of us do. Intolerance is the source of all man's misery."

Rex agreed as he gave Paige a long, considering glance. "You have to work at it, daughter. To make a marriage last, every day you have to accept something about your partner that might not please you completely."

Paige knew he was right. She had to accept the man True was, not some illusion she had built over the years. But True had come to this marriage with illusions about her, too. The main difference between them was that she had love to soften the corners and ease the way. What did he have to help him accept her?

Tartly, Tillie said, "Seems to me you can't work on a marriage when you're not at home with your man."

Sighing, Paige replied, "All right, I'll go home if that's what you want."

"It's not what I want that's important."

"Since when?" Paige demanded, laughing.

Tillie chuckled with her, then rose to go to the kitchen and wrap up some leftover pie for the twins and True.

Paige bent to kiss her father on the cheek. "Thanks, Dad. I needed to hear some wise words from you tonight."

He caught her hand again. "Was this just a newlywed tiff, or are you and True in trouble?"

Even though trouble seemed too severe a term to apply to the state of her marriage, she couldn't lie to her father completely, either. "We rushed into this marriage. We might have grown up together, but there's a lot we didn't know about each other. It wouldn't have hurt to wait."

After a moment of quiet contemplation, Rex asked, "Do you love True?"

Her answer took no thought. "With all my heart."

"Even with the faults you're discovering in him?"

She gave that some consideration, but still came up with the same result. True was the only man she could imagine living with, loving, making a home with. "I loved him after he married someone else," she told her father quietly. "So I guess I can love him no matter what."

"Then show him."

Her smile was wobbly. "I don't know if that's enough, Dad."

"But it's your best shot." Rex squeezed her fingers. "I'm always here, you know."

In the kitchen, in her own awkward and plain-spoken way, Tillie gave Paige the same reassurances.

Later, as she drove carefully through the rain that was indeed turning to ice, Paige reflected on how lucky she was to have her father and the practical housekeeper who had helped raise her. Tillie had never tried to take her mother's place, but she had always been there. As for Rex... Paige smiled. After growing up under his roof, it was no wonder she had a thing for big, tough Texas males.

As for the man waiting under the Circle W ranch house roof, Paige resolved to exercise some more patience. Even if he didn't love her, they had a common history and had made the ultimate commitment to each other. With all that going for them, they could surely work out their problems.

An unusual number of lights were burning at the house and down at the barn when Paige came up the driveway. She got out of her car quickly, worried that something was wrong. Her fears intensified when she found the house empty. It was Friday night, and the twins were allowed to stay up late, but it was getting on toward eleven o'clock. Where was everyone?

Heart pounding, she dialed the ranch office extension number, but got no answer. So she plunged outside again and headed for the barns, sleet stinging her cheeks and catching in her uncovered hair.

Outside the stables, she noticed Gray Nolan's Jeep. Just inside the door, she ran into one of the ranch hands and demanded to know what was going on.

Billy appeared around a corner before the man could answer and told her, "Poppy's foal is coming. Right now."

Infected by his excitement, Paige took his hand and hurried toward the far end of the stable.

Chapter Ten

Paige knew she would remember the night Poppy's foal was born as the night she started loving True's daughter.

From the start, Billy had been easy to love. Maybe it was that he was so much like his father, or that his smile was so ready, or that even when he was being a brat, he had a roguish charm. With Billy, you knew where you stood.

Becca was a more complicated personality, and she gave back only portions of the affection Paige had tried to offer her. Paige thought she understood Becca. Certainly, she sympathized with her. She loved her on some level just because she was True's daughter. But as for loving her just for herself, Paige hadn't been so sure about that.

Until this night.

The minute Paige came near the stall where the horse was down, she knew Poppy was in trouble. As she took in the low, tense male voices on the other side of the partition, she realized Gray's vehicle outside should have tipped her off. Most normal births on this ranch didn't call for the services of a veterinarian.

And if she had needed any further confirmation of complications, Paige had only to look at Becca's white, set face.

The girl was standing just outside the open stall door, hands clasped. She turned wide, terror-stricken eyes toward Paige and Billy as they approached, then refocused her attention on the activity surrounding her favorite horse.

Billy regarded his sister with concern. "What's happening?"

"Daddy says the baby's turned wrong," she replied.

Paige laid her hand on Becca's shoulder. "Calm down, now. That happens a lot. Gray and your daddy know what to do."

Even as she uttered those comforting words, Paige looked in the stall and met True's eyes. He was at the horse's head, and in his gaze, she could see the panic. Poppy was thrashing around, in obvious distress, her long legs striking out blindly while Gray attempted to assist her foal into the world.

Assessing the situation quickly, Paige grasped Becca's hand. "Poppy needs you."

The little girl looked surprised and more than a little frightened as Paige thrust her into the stall.

True barked, "Becca needs to get out of here."

But Paige saw it otherwise. "Becca can help calm this horse. She loves Poppy, and she's the best one to be with her right now."

True protested, but Paige insisted, and Becca was installed at her father's side at Poppy's head.

There, she stroked and soothed, sang and cajoled. And Poppy's struggles eased, almost as if she had been waiting for her best friend to appear at her side. Calmer now, she allowed Gray to help her.

Paige drew back into the corridor with Billy, letting the mare, the men and Becca do their work. And it was while watching the girl's face, in seeing her wonder and joy at the birth of the foal, that Paige's heart melted. There was so much tenderness hidden beneath this child's controlled little exterior. So much love.

At that moment, staring at Becca, with Billy's hand clutched hard in hers, Paige realized she was lucky to know these kids and to be part of their lives. Whatever else True might have offered her with their marriage, this opportunity with these children was a precious gift. She hoped she could remember that when the frustrations of everyday life threatened to overwhelm them.

Poppy had a strong little boy, with a white star on his forehead to match his mother's. Becca instantly christened him Starbright.

"Oh, Daddy," she breathed, staring in rapt adoration at the foal. "Isn't he beautiful? Didn't Poppy do good?"

But True wasn't paying much attention to Poppy's offspring. He was more impressed with his own, with this fierce little girl who had waded in to a frightening situation and helped. He reached out and touched Becca's cheek, his voice raw with emotion and pride. "You're the one who did good."

Gray added, "Miss Whitman, you can assist me anytime."

Beaming, Becca patted the neck of the exhausted mare. But when Poppy seemed ready to let her go, the girl went out in the corridor, straight to Paige. And she hugged her. Hard.

"I'm glad you pushed me in there," she told a surprised-looking Paige.

"I think you saved the day," Paige said huskily. She was blinking rapidly. "I'm really proud."

Even Billy had to pat Becca on the back and give her some credit.

True traded a long look with Paige. He realized he should be elated. His daughter and wife were becoming close. As a bonus, Becca had helped avert a possible disaster with an expensive horse and the foal who represented an important investment to the ranch's fledgling horse-breeding program.

But ever since Paige had raced out of the house earlier tonight, True had felt empty. Sad. Like he was failing, somehow. Failing Paige. Failing his children.

This incident with Becca and the horse only reinforced that sensation. It had been Paige who knew Becca could calm the mare, and Paige who had insisted that she try. He felt like a bystander.

Two months ago, he had sought marriage, hoping

to make his life complete. Instead of completion, however, he found himself falling short of the mark.

But he didn't know what to do to change it.

The time was well past three before True walked away from the stable. Paige had coerced the children to bed more than an hour ago, almost dragging Becca bodily away from Poppy and her foal.

Outside, True was happy to see the rain and ice had stopped falling. The temperature, however, was now plummeting. Weathermen were predicting a major early March storm to move into West Texas by Sunday. Sighing, True gazed at the ring around the moon and had to agree with the forecast. He could only pray the bad weather wouldn't adversely affect his cattle.

A sound caught his attention, and he looked up to find Paige coming down the graveled driveway, carrying a thermos in one hand and a blanket in the other.

"I was afraid something was wrong when you didn't come in," she explained. "I thought you might want some caffeine and some company."

"I waited to make sure Poppy and her boy were settled in for the night."

"Then you're coming to bed?"

He nodded, and an awkward silence fell as their breaths formed clouds in the cold air.

Finally, Paige murmured, "I'm sorry I left earlier tonight. I went and had dinner with Dad and Tillie."

True nodded.

"I shouldn't have walked away. That's exactly what I fussed at you for."

He turned toward the house. He was far too weary

to engage in any more battles with Paige tonight. She seemed to sense he needed the space. They went to bed without exchanging more than a few more words.

It was much later than usual when True awakened, and he blinked at the pale light beyond the bedroom's drawn curtains. Paige was curled at his side, one hand on his chest, her head pillowed against his arm. She was warm and soft, her hair smelling of her perfume. He took in a deep breath. It hadn't taken long for her favorite scent to become familiar to him. Familiar, and yet always exciting, even now, when he didn't want to notice.

She stirred, groaning. "Tell me it's not morning."

She said the same thing every day, no matter what time they arose. True had to smile. "But it is. Seven o'clock, too. We're late."

She groaned again, and reached out to stop him when he shifted away in preparation for getting up. "Stay here for just a moment. Let me hold you."

He stayed. On another day, he might have turned over, touched her, kissed her. They would make love. Today, however, True lay still. In the past few weeks, deciding to have sex with Paige had been uncomplicated. He wanted. She wanted. So they did.

Now, however, everything felt much more complex. If they made love right now, Paige might tell him she loved him. If she did, he would feel guilty. If she didn't, he would think of all the shortcomings she obviously found in him.

The confusing state of their relationship caused a knot in his neck. While he knew the simplest thing he could do would be to talk to her, he wasn't entirely sure what he would say.

So instead of giving in to her warmth, True got up and eased his tension under a pounding shower. When he was dressed, he found Paige, in jeans and a red sweater, already in the kitchen with the children.

She was busy, cooking bacon and eggs, her one specialty in the kitchen. While True poured himself coffee and Billy filled juice glasses, Becca made toast. They ate, and True was grateful for the kids' bright chatter about last night's exciting events. He could feel Paige watching him, her gaze faintly troubled, but he wasn't up to idle conversation.

Then she mentioned going into town to pick up the wallpaper and paint she had selected for their bedroom and sitting area.

True cleared his throat. "Could you hold off on that?"

"How come? I thought we decided on the color and patterns last weekend."

"I don't want us to do that work right now."

Her brow knit in a frown. "Why?"

He glanced at the kids, who were listening to every word. Normally, he didn't talk much about money in front of them, but Paige seemed to think he should be more open. She was right about so many things, perhaps he should do as she suggested.

"We can't afford to do any remodeling right now," he said, his voice gruffer than he intended.

Slowly, Paige set her coffee mug to the side. "It's not that expensive, True."

"But it's not a good time. I want to see how the

herd shapes up. With this bad weather moving in, we may have some losses. They're talking about heavy snow, and that could mean more repairs to the outbuildings.''

There was a moment of silence, the tension palpable in the room. True saw Becca's eyes widen as she looked from Paige to him and back again. Billy shifted in his seat. At the opposite end of the table, he could see Paige struggling to hold her tongue.

Finally, she lost the battle. Chin tilted, she said, ''I don't suppose it would do any good for me to offer to buy the supplies we need.''

His answer was a flat ''No.''

''Even though it's my room, as well, and I have a right to make it as pleasant as I want?''

True placed his fork and knife across his plate and exhaled. ''I don't see why you can't wait a month or so.''

She fixed him with a smoldering gaze. ''This is silly.''

True secretly agreed, but he couldn't seem to stop himself. Why did she have to push matters so often?

Chair legs scraped across the floor as he pushed himself back from the table. He wasn't staying here to argue, especially not in front of Becca and Billy. ''I'm going out. There's a lot to do before this storm hits.''

''I'm sure there is,'' Paige said, heavy on the sarcasm.

Ignoring her, True gave some instructions to the children about some chores for the day.

Becca said, "I'm going to check on Poppy and Starbright first, okay?"

Remembering that Paige thought he let the kids weasel out of responsibilities, True gave his daughter a stern look. "You do your chores first." He swiveled his gaze to Billy before the boy could give his sister a gloating smile. "And you, too."

Nobody at the table moved or said a word as he put on his coat and gloves, grabbed up his hat and went outside.

But Paige caught him on the porch. "I know you're angry at me about last night, but you don't have to take it out on Becca and Billy."

"I'm not angry," True said, shoving his hat on his head.

"You look angry."

"I look tired," he retorted. "Which is what I am. I'm tired and I've got more work than I can do, and I'm not getting it done by standing here having a pointless conversation with you. Or by arguing about paint and wallpaper."

Shivering against the cold, she said, "You make me want to scream. You're mad as hell at me and you can't even admit it."

"Sorry I can't articulate my feelings better for you," he mocked, mouth twisting bitterly. "You should have realized what you were getting when you married me."

"I could say the same thing to you."

"Oh, really?" True drawled, a hollow feeling in his gut. "Lately, I've been thinking neither one of us

had a clue what we were getting into.'' Then he
stalked away, boots crunching on the frozen ground.

Long after he had disappeared down the ranch road
to the barns, Paige stood in the cold. She felt as if he
had smacked her across the jaw. What else could she
feel when he had as good as told her he wished they
hadn't married?

Behind her, the door creaked open. In a small
voice, Billy said, ''Are you okay?''

Determinedly, she blinked her tears away and
turned to face him. ''Of course.''

''Then why are you standing out here?''

''Just thinking,'' she said, following him back into
the warm and brightly cheerful kitchen. The gray and
overcast outdoors was much more suited to her mood.

True's final words to her echoed in Paige's head
all day. She cleaned the kitchen and did laundry. She
heated some soup Tillie had sent over for lunch and
left it on the stove for True and the kids while she
went into Amarillo to do the grocery shopping. It was
afternoon before she completed an assortment of other
errands and made it back to the ranch.

The predicted weather seemed poised to break over
them. Clouds were thickening in the west, and the
wind blowing from the north. The phone rang while
Paige was putting groceries away. It was her father,
saying he could feel the snow coming in his bones.
A big one, he predicted.

Paige purposely kept her tone light and happy during the call. She knew her father was really calling to
see if she was okay, and though she was far from

being fine, she didn't want to talk about it right now. Like she had told Billy this morning, she needed to think.

But any consideration of what she could do about the situation with True brought his bitter words to mind. He hadn't known what he was getting into by marrying her. That made her head ache and her stomach clench.

There were a couple of dozen tasks she could complete here in the house, but Paige couldn't stand the thought of them. She wanted to be outside. Or at least in the barn, grooming a horse or spreading fresh hay in the stalls.

She gravitated naturally toward the stables where the mother and new son were. As she expected, she heard Becca and Billy's voices the minute she walked inside.

True and an older man he introduced as Ned Waite were in the stall with Poppy and Starbright. The kids were seated in one corner, watching Starbright enjoy a meal.

"Ned owns this fella's sire," True explained to Paige, nodding at the unsteady little foal. "He called this morning to see if Poppy had foaled and decided to drive over and see the outcome."

"And a fine outcome it is," Ned said, casting an approving look over Starbright. The two men joined Paige in the corridor outside the stall, and Ned glanced at True, his eyes shrewd. "I might just make you an offer for this one."

"I might be listening, if the figure's right," True replied, crossing his arms. He looked much the way

Paige's father did before he began to negotiate for a
bull, a piece of machinery or a tract of land.

Ned named a sum that Paige could hardly believe.

If True was impressed, he gave nothing of his reactions away. He leaned back against the stall door
opposite Poppy's and rubbed his chin. Finally, he
said, "That would be close."

Ned upped the ante.

True stuck out his hand. "You've got yourself a
new horse."

Over the men's joined hands, Paige saw Becca
standing in Poppy's stall doorway. The shock on the
girl's face made Paige suck in her breath. The sound
got True's attention.

He looked at his daughter, and all color drained
from his cheeks. He took a step toward her.

She was shaking her head. "You can't sell him.
Daddy, you can't sell Poppy's baby."

"Becca, honey," he said, reaching her side. "You
know Poppy is part of our business here, just like the
cattle are part of the ranch business."

Her voice rose. "But I thought Poppy was mine.
You never said you'd sell her foal. You never told
me."

He put his hands on her shoulders. "I thought you
knew."

"But you never said." Twisting away from her father, Becca glared at Ned Waite, her voice rising to
a shout. "You can't have my foal. I won't let you
have her."

Looking uncomfortable, the older man shifted from
foot to foot. "Honey, now—"

"It's okay, Ned," True cut in. He speared Becca with a glance. "You apologize."

Tears were now streaming down the girl's face. But she stood her ground, face red, hands clenched into fists at her sides, shaking her head. Paige could almost hear Becca's heart breaking.

True's jaw clenched as he repeated, "You apologize and then get up to the house."

Stubbornly, Becca shook her head again.

And Paige found herself unable to just stand there. "True, can't we talk about this?"

His look was sharp enough to sever her head. "No, we can't."

But Ned said, "Now, True, maybe—"

"Don't worry about this," True told him, another grim glance at Paige. "My daughter's a little upset. But a deal's a deal, and the foal is yours. Let me walk you to your car."

When their footsteps faded, the stable was filled with the nickers of horses, the faint swishing tails and tossing of manes. Then Becca started to sob.

Throwing herself into the straw in the corner of Poppy's stall, she wailed. Great, gut-wrenching cries that tore at Paige's insides. The mare felt the girl's distress, as well. Eyes rolling, she shifted about, trying to guard her foal.

It took both Paige and Billy to get Becca out of the stall and away from the increasingly agitated horse.

Then True appeared at the end of the corridor and Becca pulled away and ran to him. "Please, Daddy. Please don't do it."

He caught her shoulders, then knelt down in front

of her. He cupped her face between his hands. "There's nothing else to say about this, Becca. You might as well calm down. These horses are not your pets."

"But Poppy's different."

"No, she's not. We make a living selling horses and cattle. And that's final."

Angrily, Becca pushed herself away from him. "Starbright's more important than money. He belongs with me and Poppy."

Paige tried to intervene. "Honey, the foal will get to stay here until Poppy's ready for him to go."

But Becca was having none of what Paige could offer, either. Face twisted with anger and pain, she said, "What do you care? When Daddy gets the money for Starbright, then you can do over the house. Everybody can have what they want except me."

The words were a defense mechanism, the typical striking out of a child in distress, but with them, Paige saw some of the progress she had made with Becca come crashing down. Still, she tried to reach the girl, only Becca wasn't interested in her comfort. Coat flapping, she ran down the stable corridor, disappearing into the cold, late-afternoon air.

For once not taking off after her, Billy stood at Paige's side, his face pinched and white.

Straightening up, True nodded toward the house. "You go on up, too," he told his son. Billy trudged reluctantly away, and Paige started to follow. She didn't have anything to say to True at this moment.

But he caught her arm before she could leave. His

tone low, he said, "I don't appreciate you undercutting me with the kids."

"Undercutting?"

"I told her to apologize and go up to the house. She had no business being rude to Ned."

"She was upset."

"But that's no call to cause a scene."

"She's just a child, and you're taking away a horse that she thought was hers."

"She knew it wasn't hers."

"She said she didn't."

"That's just an excuse to try to get her way. She has to learn she can't always."

"But is this the way to teach her?"

True blew out a frustrated breath. "Damnation, Paige. Last night you said I was too easy on her. Now you're criticizing me for some discipline."

Paige jerked her arm out of his grasp. "You call this discipline?"

He threw up his hands and shouted, "I don't know what to call anything anymore, I guess. You've got me so confused I can't do anything right. Or least not to suit you."

"Don't put this on me."

He sucked in his breath. "This is ridiculous. We run a ranch here. Becca has to learn not to get so attached to these animals. Some of them won't stay. I know that's a lesson I had to learn. It's one your father taught you."

"But my father never sold a horse I loved right in front of me. My father would never treat me like that."

Paige didn't pause to see what effect that statement had on True. She stalked away, coming around the corner of the stalls and toward the door just in time to see Billy dart away. He had been listening, she realized, listening to her and True argue.

Knowing he was probably upset, she called for him, but he had disappeared among the many outbuildings.

With a weary sigh, she went up to a cold, silent house. It matched her spirit.

Chapter Eleven

A winter storm came charging across the plains early Sunday, and as Rex Whitman had predicted, it was a big one. Nearly a foot of snow, driving winds and subfreezing temperatures. On Tuesday, however, the thermometer shot up again, causing a major melt. Spring arrived with its usual intensity.

Everywhere except in True's household. There, it was deep-freeze.

Becca had adopted a chilly, almost surreally calm manner. She avoided the stables and her father with almost equal zeal.

True, the man who hated conflict, thought he would prefer another screaming outburst from her. A dozen times he started to talk to her about Poppy, to explain his decision, to apologize. Then he thought of Paige's criticism of his handling of the matter, and he dug in his heels. Paige was more on the mark when she had accused him of being too easy with the children. Did he need to apologize to his ten-year-old daughter for conducting ranch business? His own father wouldn't have. And despite Paige's outburst, he doubted Rex McMullen would have gone all soft with her.

In typical twin fashion, Billy had fallen in line with Becca. He was quiet, almost subdued. He spent a lot of time down at the stables, tending to Poppy and Starbright, as if making up for Becca's neglect.

As for Paige...well, True decided the old adage about being careful what you wished for was correct. Since the afternoon he had sold Starbright, she had been much more the wife he had supposed he was getting when he said "I do."

Though Jenny had indeed started work as soon as the weather broke, Paige had no trouble getting home from the Double M in time to meet the twins' bus.

A hot meal was on the table every night when True came in.

There were no demands.

No criticisms.

No arguments.

Each evening, when he opened the door and stepped inside, True knew exactly what to expect. The days no longer contained a sharp anticipatory edge.

There was no edge at all.

No "I love you" notes stuck to the bathroom mirror.

No waking him up in the middle of the night just to tell him her latest great idea for new entertainment for the dudes this summer.

No racing each other to the bedroom as soon as the twins were out for the night.

No lingering in the warm covers in the mornings.

Not that Paige denied him anything. When he turned to her in bed midway through the first week of the big chill, she met his kisses with eagerness. She took him inside her body with pliant, supple grace.

But she was quiet afterward. Quiet, where she used to be ready to talk. Ready to be with him again. And again.

Was this really the wife he had wished for?

On a Thursday afternoon, while spring thunder rumbled in the distance, True sat in the ranch office, staring at a computer screen. For hours he had been trying to concentrate on income and expense projections while his ranch hands were out doing what he really enjoyed. Surely life was simpler when a man just raised the beef, prayed for good prices and then took what he could get.

A simple life. The words brought a rueful chuckle. Had there ever been such a thing? Surely dealings between men and women made that impossible.

The scrape of the door opening made him look up. Paige hesitated in the doorway. He hated that. She should have come storming in, smiling, plopping down in his lap. That was Paige of only a few weeks ago. This was the person who had taken her place.

"Have you seen the kids?" she asked.

"Aren't they home from school?"

"I was running a few minutes late, but they weren't at the house when I got in."

True checked his wristwatch. "It's half past four. Are you sure they're not out for a ride?"

Paige bit her lip. He got the feeling there was something she wasn't telling him. He waited.

She cleared her throat. "Poppy and Starbright aren't in their stall or the corral."

He blinked. "So you're saying the kids have taken them out somewhere?"

She nodded but said nothing, her eyes very somber.

Her silence sent the worst implications of the twins' absence clicking into place in True's brain. He stood quickly. "Did you just now check the stable?"

"It was a half hour ago."

He frowned at her. "And you're just now telling me?"

"I didn't think much about it until I couldn't find them by checking the fields closest to home."

True swore and clicked off the computer with an impatient move. "They've taken off with those horses." Thunder rumbled again, much closer now. "When it's about to storm. They've run off to do something foolish, haven't they?"

"I don't want to think so, but both of them have been upset about this. I've been afraid—"

"Then why didn't you come get me when you first found the horses and the kids gone?" *And why hadn't he been paying attention when he knew how badly both kids were feeling?*

Temper flashed in her eyes—a glimmer of the Paige he was used to, quickly subdued but still showing in her gaze.

He told himself to calm down and think about

where the twins might have gone. "I'll bet anything they're off looking for that hidden canyon again."

"Probably," Paige agreed, looking miserable. "I'm sorry, True, sorry I was late. But I got hung up and I didn't think—"

"Forget it," he said, much harsher than he intended. He wasn't blaming her for this, not any more than he blamed himself. He should have seen it coming. He cleared his throat. "I'll go get them. It shouldn't be hard to catch up."

"I'll go with you."

"No, I'll do this."

His terse order cut Paige to the core. She wanted to protest, to insist on coming. But she knew True wouldn't appreciate that. Since the night this had started, she had been schooling herself to hold her temper and curb her impulsiveness, to be the sort of person she felt True wanted her to be. Sometimes she thought she was going to explode. But if she wanted this marriage, she had to adjust. While it was one thing to be true to herself, some of her traits were not welcomed by this man. Surely learning to compromise wouldn't kill her.

So she stood to the side while he headed out to the horse she had saddled and ridden in her first quick search for the twins. He rode away without a backward glance.

Her legs were so heavy it was difficult to drag herself to the house.

Once there, she faced the emptiness and a dozen, jumbled questions.

Why hadn't she been home when Becca and Billy got off the bus?

Why hadn't she seen that they were plotting something?

More importantly, why had she been silent these past few weeks? Silent, when she knew that all they needed—her, True and the kids—was to face this subject about the foal and talk it through.

Why had she done this True's usual way, which was to ignore a problem in hopes it would disappear?

Anger at herself increased. As an hour ticked by, the storm outside broke in sheets of rain, thunder and lightning. The phone rang once, a short quick ring. But it was dead when Paige picked up the receiver. The lights flickered once and went out, as well. Darkness fell as the storm blew itself out with the customary suddenness of most spring squalls.

Paige lit the oil lamp on the mantel. Then she carried it with her as she prowled restlessly through the house. She went from window to window, peering out, and damning herself for everything she had and hadn't done since she had married True and became part of his children's lives.

She was so mad she wanted to spit. To throw things. In the sitting room next to her bedroom, Paige glanced wildly about, searching for some object which would take the brunt of her anger. Her gaze fell on the ugly, green-flocked wallpaper that she hated intensely. The wallpaper that was still up on these walls because True was a stubborn, macho throwback to a prehistoric era in which men were supposed to pay for everything.

Setting the lamp aside, Paige tore into that wallpaper with her bare hands. It wasn't so hard since the sad stuff was sagging in several places, torn in others, yellowed and brittle in others.

She ripped and tore and cursed and cried.

While she did it, she imagined she was flailing at all the childish illusions she had brought to this marriage.

The hope that she could make True happy.

And the long-buried wish that he would learn to love her.

That was it, she realized. That was all she had ever wanted. She could lie to herself about it, but deep, deep in her heart she had placed that hopeless desire. That was why she had been trying so hard to change herself these past few weeks. She wanted to be the sort of person True could love.

But she wasn't that kind of person. She never could be. True would never love her. And without that love, she might as well give up on this marriage. She couldn't live with half measures.

With vicious anger, she tore at a stubborn swath of paper. Her fingers were bleeding. She was trembling. And she couldn't get hold of this patch. Like she couldn't get hold of her heart's desire.

Choking back a sob, Paige fell to her knees in the middle of the mess she had created. She sat there, rocking, until the lights came back on.

From the doorway, True said, "What are you doing?"

Tears clearing, Paige jumped up and demanded, "Where are the kids?"

He shook his head as he doffed his wet poncho. "When I didn't catch up with them in an hour, I knew they hadn't gone to the canyon. I've got the rest of the hands out looking now."

"I've got to go, too," she said, starting forward.

But True caught her. Gently, he lifted one raw, bleeding hand. Eyes glittering with an emotion she couldn't name, he looked at her fingers, then back at her. "What have you done to yourself?" He glanced around. "And this room?"

"I've ruined it," she retorted, snatching her hand back. "Ruined it the same as I've ruined our lives." Biting her lip to keep from going on, she tried to brush past him.

"No," he said, catching her again. "You tell me what you mean by that?"

"True, we've got to go find the children."

"Are the children the only reason you tore this paper down, the reason you're sitting in the middle of the room, crying?"

"Yes...no." She struggled to get free. "Just let me go, True. Let's find the children and then we'll talk."

"I want to talk now, about why you think your life is ruined." There was a hitch in his voice; a muscle jumped beneath his eye. "Have I ruined your life, Paige?"

"I ruined it," she said, struggling with her tears. "I married you, knowing that I loved you and you didn't love me. And then everything I did made you miserable."

"No," True protested, framing her face with his hands. "You didn't make me miserable. I did that."

But she wasn't listening to him. "I'm not anything like Marcie."

"I don't want you to be."

"But you loved her."

"And she's gone."

"But you wanted someone like her."

"I thought I did." With wonder beginning to dawn inside him, True searched Paige's tearstained features. The pert, freckled nose. The stubborn chin. The brown eyes like velvet. The blond hair with its hint of wildcat red.

He had seen her as a girl. As a friend. As a woman. In sadness. In mirth. In pain. In passion.

But why in the hell had he never seen how much he loved her?

Just her. Just exactly as she was.

Carefully, he slipped his hands from her face to her shoulders. Painstakingly, he formed the words he wanted to say. "I don't want you to be anyone but you."

"But I make you crazy."

"Yeah, but you also make me feel alive."

She was staring at him, her mouth trembling.

He put his arms around her. "I love you, Paige McMullen Whitman. It may have taken me too damn long to figure it out. But I love you."

He kissed her. With all the joy and discovery and wonder that was winging through his heart. Funny how love made that kiss sweeter than all those that had come before.

They were still kissing when a horn sounded outside.

"The kids," Paige finally murmured, breaking away. "It might be the kids."

And it was.

Outside was one of the Double M's trucks with a horse trailer attached. Tillie was driving.

The older woman stuck her head out the driver's window as Paige and True spilled down the porch steps. "Are you two missing some children and horses?"

"Are they all right?" Paige demanded.

"All four of 'em are just fine," Tillie replied.

Peering in the truck cab, True found his apprehensive-looking son and daughter snuggled in between Tillie and Rex.

Beside him, Paige suggested, "Let's get Poppy and Starbright to the stable before we discuss this."

True let Becca and Billy unload the mare and son while Rex explained that the twins had turned up at his ranch about the time the lights had gone out. The phone being out as well was the reason he and Tillie had just brought them home.

Coming out of the stall, a contrite-looking Billy explained, "I remembered what you said, Paige."

She was confused. "What I said about what?"

"That your father would never sell your horse."

True was still confused until Paige told him, "Billy heard us arguing the afternoon you sold Starbright. He heard what I said about my father."

The boy nodded. "So I figured Mr. Whitman might help us." He turned as his sister came out of the stall. "Today, when Paige wasn't home when we got off the bus, I talked Becca into taking the horses. We took turns walking and riding.''

''And I've decided to help them,'' Rex said, stepping in between the youngsters. He fixed True with a firm look while he leaned on his cane. Becca slipped an arm through his. ''I'm offering you double what Ned Waite's willing to pay for Starbright. And then...'' He looked down at Becca and winked. ''Then I'm giving him to my granddaughter.''

Tillie sniffed and wiped her eyes. Paige had pressed a hand to her mouth.

But True shook his head. ''I can't do it,'' he said to Rex.

Becca's eyes rounded and Billy's head went down. True stepped up to them both. ''I can't do it,'' he whispered. ''Because this foal already belongs to somebody.''

True had to give his daughter credit. She held on to her tears, though her chin trembled. Very slowly, she nodded. ''You already sold him to Mr. Waite.''

''No,'' True murmured, reaching out to stroke her cheek. ''This horse isn't being sold to anyone until you say so. He belongs to you.''

When Becca flung herself into his arms, it was the second-best feeling True had had all day. He grinned at Paige over his daughter's head, not surprised to see she was crying. He had a feeling he would have to get used to that sight. Being in love with and married to an emotional firecracker meant there would be plenty of tears around this place. And lots of laughter.

And he was going to count himself lucky either way.

Drawing back from Becca, True said to her and her brother, "I'm not saying what you did today was smart, but it got my attention. You want this horse, don't you?"

They nodded their heads.

"Then you've got him. And I promise that you won't have to pull something like this again to make me pay attention. I'm going to try harder."

Paige slipped an arm around his waist. "If you try, I think all of us will be willing to cut you some slack."

"That's a deal, Slim."

Epilogue

Sitting on the top rung of a fence down by the barns, Paige tipped her head back and reveled in the warm May sunshine on her face. She felt as content and lazy as a house cat.

In the corral, Becca and Billy were putting their horses through some paces. True had entered them in a junior trick riding competition this Saturday. Paige had a feeling they would come home with some ribbons.

Life was perfect, she decided, watching Billy do a rolling dismount.

No, not perfect.

The self-correction made her smile. Perfection, she had come to realize, was an illusion. As foolish as the dreams she had once had about marrying True.

Reality was a little tougher. She was married to a

man, not a dream. Someone who could be stubborn and dogmatic. A man who had to work hard to express his feelings. Who clung to some old-fashioned notions about a woman's place. But he was learning. He was trying.

And he loved her.

She hugged that knowledge to herself. True was being great, considering how much he had to put up with from her. She had a tendency to want to take things over, and she was every bit as stubborn as him. And she was hard on herself. True had helped her realize this last fact. She was trying to ease up, not get upset when she had to give less than her all to the Double M or True and the children. It was amazing how her insecurities and frustrations eased when he looked at her in his special, True way and told her he loved her.

Love—now that was perfect.

And this family she and True were forming, it had potential for near-flawlessness. True was listening more to his children, seeing them as individuals instead of a matched set. And the ties between Paige and the twins were strengthening daily, as well. Becca, especially, was reaching out to her.

A horse nickered behind her, and Paige turned to find True with a long-legged Starbright ambling after him.

"You two need to come enjoy the show," Paige said with a smile. "The kids are looking great."

"Just so long as you don't get any bright ideas about getting out there with them," True said. "Not like last week."

Mockingly, Paige replied, "Yes, master."

"I know you think I'm being overprotective."

"And if this is the way it's going to be—"

A horn blowing interrupted her. Paige recognized Gray Nolan's Jeep pulling in next to the stables. But Gray didn't appear to be alone.

"Kathryn's brought the baby," she said, jumping off the fence and racing toward the car.

True hollered a protest after her, but she didn't stop until she greeted her old friend and got her hands on two-month-old Lily Nolan.

Pressing her cheek to the baby's dark, downy hair, Paige gushed, "She's grown every time I see her."

Like the proud parents they were, Gray and Kathryn beamed.

True, who had been forced to stop and tether Starbright to the fence, finally reached them. Without even greeting their visitors, he told Paige, "You need to stop jumping off fences."

"And you need to stop being ridiculous," Paige said, still cooing over the baby. She slanted a glance at Kathryn.

Her friend looked at her for a moment, then squealed and hugged her, baby and all.

Gray looked confused.

Grinning broadly, True explained, "You remember that bet you made with Paige's father at our wedding? Well...it'll be close, but we might have a baby by Christmas. I can't guarantee it'll be a boy, though."

Gray slapped him on the back and shook his hand.

Paige laughed at True's goofy smile. He had been walking around this way for the past month, when she finally realized that a slipup in March had resulted in a baby. They had been thrilled, but they had waited to share the news. Neither of them had breathed easy until the twins had been told. They had done that just last night, and the results had been great. Despite her earlier proclamation, Becca said she was looking forward to the baby.

Today they had told everyone else. Paige's father had done a jig around his cane. Tillie had cried. Over the phone, Aunt Helen had cackled and offered an emphatic "I knew it wouldn't be long!"

Paige handed Lily back to Kathryn. "True's driving me crazy. Treating me like I'm made of glass or something."

"Enjoy it," her friend advised, jiggling the fussing infant. "He'll decide you're plenty tough about the third night in a row that the baby wakes you up screaming."

They all laughed. True slipped his arm around Paige and tried to defend his overprotectiveness. She nestled back against him, secretly very pleased at his attentiveness and concern. She really wouldn't have expected anything else from a Texas man.

Her Texas man.

Over by the fence, Billy and Becca stood with Starbright, listening to the adults.

Becca stroked her horse's neck thoughtfully. "You know, Billy, I think I know what I'm going to give Paige and Daddy's baby when he's born."

Billy rubbed his chin. "You have to give him something?"

"Everybody gives a gift when there's a baby, silly." She grinned. "I think I'll give him Starbright."

For a moment Billy looked at her in astonishment. Then he smiled, in perfect agreement, before the two of them swung back over the fence to resume their practice.

* * * * *

DIANA PALMER
ANN MAJOR
SUSAN MALLERY

RETURN TO WHITEHORN

In **April 1998** get ready to catch the bouquet. Join in the excitement as these bestselling authors lead us down the aisle with three heartwarming tales of love and matrimony in Big Sky country.

A very engaged lady is having second thoughts about her intended; a pregnant librarian is wooed by the town bad boy; a cowgirl meets up with her first love. Which Maverick will be the next one to get hitched?

Available in **April 1998.**

Silhouette's beloved **MONTANA MAVERICKS** returns in Special Edition and Harlequin Historicals starting in February 1998, with brand-new stories from your favorite authors.

Round up these great new stories at your favorite retail outlet.

Take 4 bestselling love stories FREE
Plus get a FREE surprise gift!

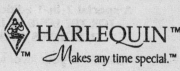

Return to the Towers!

In March
New York Times bestselling author

NORA ROBERTS

brings us to the Calhouns' fabulous
Maine coast mansion and reveals the
tragic secrets hidden there for generations.

For all his degrees, Professor Max Quartermain has a
lot to learn about love—and luscious Lilah Calhoun is
just the woman to teach him. Ex-cop Holt Bradford is
as prickly as a thornbush—until Suzanna Calhoun's
special touch makes love blossom in his heart.
And all of them are caught in the race to solve
the generations-old mystery of a priceless
lost necklace...and a timeless love.

Lilah and Suzanna
THE
Calhoun Women

A special 2-in-1 edition containing
FOR THE LOVE OF LILAH and
SUZANNA'S SURRENDER

Available at your favorite retail outlet.